THE GRIM JOKER

Mr. Hamilton Lorne is amused to receive a card with the grotesque picture of a fool, complete with cap and bells, one finger pointing at the holder. He and Superintendent Budd of Scotland Yard laugh at the threatening limerick scrawled across the back, assuming it is a feeble practical joke, and drop the card into a waste-paper basket. But no one is laughing when the following morning Mr. Lorne is found dead, stabbed through the heart — the first in a series of sadistic murders perpetrated by the elusive Grim Joker.

GERALD VERNER

THE GRIM JOKER

Complete and Unabridged

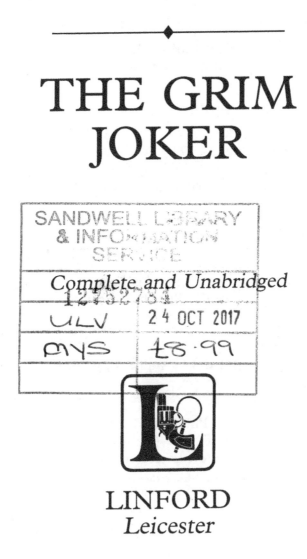

LINFORD
Leicester

First published in Great Britain

First Linford Edition
published 2017

A catalogue record for this book is available
from the British Library.

ISBN 978–1–4448–3493–2

Published by
F. A. Thorpe (Publishing)
Anstey, Leicestershire

Set by Words & Graphics Ltd.
Anstey, Leicestershire
Printed and bound in Great Britain by
T. J. International Ltd., Padstow, Cornwall

This book is printed on acid-free paper

1

The Jokes that Lacked Humour

When that stout and lethargic man, Superintendent Robert Budd, first heard of the Grim Joker, he laughed — and not without reason, for certainly the card with its grotesque picture of a fool, complete with cap and bells, one finger pointing derisively at the holder, was conducive to mirth. Mr. Hamilton Lorne, who received it by post one morning, and later showed it to Mr. Budd at the club where he had invited the latter to lunch, laughed also, particularly at the doggerel rhyme scrawled across the back:

My dear Mr. Hamilton Lorne,
You really should not have been
  born,
But to remedy this,
And be sure I shan't miss

You will die — just an hour before dawn.

Both the superintendent and Mr. Lorne, an elderly retired stockbroker, came to the conclusion that it was a feeble practical joke lacking in good taste, but a joke nevertheless. They laughed, and the recipient crumpled up the card and dropped it into the waste-paper basket.

Neither Mr. Budd nor Mr. Lorne were laughing at nine o'clock on the following morning; Mr. Budd because of the telephone message he had just received, and the stockbroker, because he was dead. He had been found in his bed by a frightened maid whose duty it was to provide him each morning with a cup of tea, and the knife that protruded from his chest testified to the manner of his death. The doctor who had been hastily called in testified that death must have taken place about an hour before dawn.

Mr. Budd heard the news calmly, and remembering the card, rubbed his many chins and wondered. It was obviously a case of murder, but neither he nor the lugubrious Sergeant Leek, who accompanied him to the scene of the crime, could find any clue offering a solution to the mystery.

The killer had entered by the bedroom window, for a light ladder used by the gardener was found leaning against the sill, and on the gravel path beneath were confused traces of blurred footprints. But that was all, and three weeks of patient enquiry failed to elicit anything further. Mr. Lorne was a bachelor and had apparently possessed few friends and no enemies. Mr. Budd, whose acquaintance with him had been of the slightest, failed to unearth anything suggesting a motive for the killing. The deceased's only living relative was a cousin who ran a sheep farm in Canada, and who, since there was no will, eventually inherited Mr. Lorne's comfortable fortune.

The newspapers, after giving a great deal of publicity to the affair and featuring the mysterious card and its grim prophecy, turned to other and more recent sensations, so that in an incredibly short space of time Mr. Lorne and his unaccountable death were forgotten, except by certain men in the large building on the Thames Embankment whose duty it was to keep a record of such things.

Then, four months later, an agitated man arrived at Scotland Yard and banged in front of Mr. Budd a square card he had received by that morning's post. It bore the figure of the fool, and on the back was written:

My dear Mr. Percival Haynes,
What a pity blood flows in your
   veins.
You'll forgive me I hope,
If I stop this with rope,
And release you from life's earthly
   pains.

The terrified Mr. Haynes, an architect who lived at Sydenham and remembered the fate of the unfortunate stockbroker, raved and threatened and implored, and eventually, being reduced to something like coherence, answered the numerous questions fired at him by the sleepy-eyed superintendent.

The card had arrived in a plain envelope, the name and address being printed in capital letters. Mr. Haynes had brought the envelope with him. The post mark showed that it had been posted in the West End of London in time for the last collection on the previous night. Mr. Budd sent both it and the card to the fingerprint department; but though there were several prints on the envelope, the card revealed nothing other than some excellent reproductions of Mr. Haynes's own fingertips.

The architect was so nervous that it was a long time before they could persuade him to leave the building, and only after he had been assured that a detective would be put on to shadow him night and day and that his house would be subjected to police surveillance. Three days passed, and Mr. Haynes never went abroad without a faithful trailer at his heels, and slept in the comfortable knowledge that a plainclothes man was somewhere near, watching for any danger that might threaten him.

In spite of these precautions, on the morning of the fourth day he walked into his garden after dinner to smoke a cigar and never came back. An anxious servant going to look for him an hour later found him hanging from the branch of a big oak tree that grew at the foot of the lawn. He was quite dead, and the watchful detective who was keeping the house under observation was found neatly chloroformed and lying unconscious in the adjoining shrubbery.

Mr. Budd uttered several unprintable words when he heard the news, and went to Sydenham as fast as a speedy police car could take him. But, as in the case of Mr. Hamilton Lorne, there was not a ghost of a clue or the slightest shadow of a motive. The only solution, it seemed, was that the crimes were the work of a homicidal maniac — a belief strengthened when, six weeks after the death of the unfortunate Percival Haynes, a third murder was blazoned forth on the front pages of the morning papers. The victim this time was an elderly spinster who lived alone in a tiny cottage on the Horsham Road.

The discovery was made by the milkman, who, finding the previous day's supply of milk still on the step and receiving no reply to his door knocking, notified the police. The door was broken open, and in the dingy sitting-room they found all that was left of Miss Julia Rothe. Her head had been battered in, and the stained and twisted poker that lay beside the body left no doubt regarding the weapon that had been used. On the little old-fashioned bureau was the now-familiar card, and across the back, in the same sprawling writing as the others, the following limerick:

Believe me, my charming Miss
    Rothe,
To end your long life I am loath.
But a blow with the poker,
In the hand of this Joker,
Will be best, I am sure, for us both.

That was all; but it was sufficient, taken in conjunction with the other two murders, to spread something very like a panic. A wave of terror swept over the country following this latest atrocious and apparently meaningless crime. The perverted sense of humour shown by the rhymed warnings that the unknown murderer sent to his intended victims, and the utter wantonness of the killing, created an atmosphere of horror that no amount of sheer brutality could have equalled. It was the very callousness — the joking way of treating carefully planned, cold-blooded murder — that seized on the public's imagination, and caused even strong-minded folk to open their morning mail with quickened heartbeats and a creeping of the flesh, lest among the letters should appear one containing the fatal picture of the laughing fool, his raised hand pointing a menacing finger at them. Mr. Budd was at his wits' end but helpless, for no amount of patient sifting, no amount of delving into the past lives of the three victims brought any results.

The Grim Joker, as the newspapers named him, had appeared from nowhere, struck swiftly and surely, and drawn back into the mists from whence he came, without leaving a single trace of his identity behind him.

Seated in his bare and cheerless office one morning, Mr. Budd read an acrimonious leader regarding the police methods in one of the popular dailies and grunted. He gave the impression of being only half-awake, but there was very little his sleepy eyes missed, for his brain was alert and, in contrast to his body, moved swiftly. There was not a cleverer detective in the whole of the C.I.D. than this bovine, lazy-looking man.

His one interest in life, apart from work, was horticulture, and it was for this reason that he had earned his nickname of Rosebud. Roses were a passion with him. The garden of his trim little villa at Streatham was ablaze throughout the summer with these flowers, and he loved nothing better than to browse among their fragrance.

He read to the end of the article, folded the newspaper carefully and laid it on his desk. 'Tripe!' he murmured, and fumbled in the pocket of his waistcoat for one of his inevitable long black cigars. He was just reaching for his matches when there came a tap on the door and a tall thin man entered carrying a folder.

'This is what you wanted,' he said, putting the folder on the desk. 'But there's nothin' in it that we didn't know before.'

Mr. Budd regarded him with half-closed eyes through the smoke of his cigar. 'Just a hunch of mine,' he said, 'and I want to verify it.' He flicked open the folder and scanned its typewritten pages.

Sergeant Leek stood by the desk and watched his superior in silence. His leanness gave an illusion of height which he did not possess, and his face was set in a permanent expression of melancholy. Although he had been at the Yard for over fifteen years, nobody could ever remember having seen him smile.

'If we could only find some suggestion of a motive for these senseless crimes,' said the Rosebud thoughtfully as he turned the pages, 'we should have somethin' to go on.'

'It's my opinion,' Sergeant Leek said, 'that these murders are the work of a lunatic. Look at them rhymes. Ridic'lous nonsense.'

'You've been readin' what the newspapers say,' grunted Mr. Budd. 'They lack imagination. Bein' sensible people, we can't entertain the maniac theory until we've exhausted everythin' else.'

'I thought we had,' murmured the sergeant.

'If you thought a little more, you'd say 'sir' now and again,' said Mr. Budd severely. 'And those rhymes aren't so ridiculous — they're very much to the point. In every instance their prediction has been carried out to the letter.'

'That may be,' said Leek stubbornly. 'But I still say this joker fellow is mad. Look at the people he's picked for his victims. A stockbroker, an architect and an old maid.' He ticked them off on the fingers of his left hand. 'Ord'nary people, without any connection between 'em.'

'That's where you're wrong,' said Mr. Budd, blowing out a cloud of smoke. 'There *is* a connection between these

11

people.' He tapped the open folder on the desk. 'If you'd take the trouble to read up all about them, you'll see what I mean.'

The sergeant had no intention of again wading through the lengthy reports. 'S'pose you tell me what it is?'

'None of them possessed any living relatives,' Mr. Budd said impressively. 'The only one of the three who had a relation of any sort was Lorne, and his Canadian cousin is so far removed that he's nearly gone altogether.'

The sergeant shrugged. 'It's odd, certainly. But I don't see how it's going to help.'

'Neither do I at the moment,' confessed the stout superintendent, 'but it may be worth remembering. I don't think we've heard the last of our joking friend, an' I'd bet that the next person to get one of those poetic effusions would be someone without livin' relatives.'

'Then you don't believe in this theory that it's the work of a lunatic?'

'Hm,' grunted the Rosebud. 'I suppose you didn't kill these people, by any chance?'

'Good Lord, no!'

'Then I don't see how they could have been done by a madman,' remarked Mr. Budd.

2

Larry Weston

The discomfited sergeant sighed. Mr. Budd had an unfortunate habit of making this kind of remark when he was irritable, but the melancholy sergeant had got used to it.

Before he could respond, there came a knock on the door and a young man entered. 'Hello. Busy?' he remarked pleasantly, grinning.

'Very,' Mr. Budd replied lazily. 'Who let you up, Mr. Weston?'

Larry Weston perched himself on the edge of the desk. 'They're beginning to know me downstairs now. I just smiled at the man at the door, mentioned your name, and he let me pass without a word.'

'Very reprehensible,' muttered the superintendent. 'Don' know what the Yard's comin' to.'

The newcomer's smile broadened.

'Have I butted in just as you were laying the plans for the arrest of some desperate criminal?'

'There's only one desperate criminal worryin' me at the moment,' Mr. Budd said sadly, 'an' we can't lay any plans to arrest him because we don't know who he is.'

The other's smile faded. 'I suppose you mean the limerick man?' he said seriously. 'I was talking about him to Dr. Roone the other day. His idea is that the fellow's a lunatic.'

'From what I can gather, that seems to be the popular theory,' grunted Mr. Budd a little wearily. 'Whenever somebody does somethin' what isn't just ordinary and conventional, people immediately jump to the conclusion that he's mad. Must be because they haven't any originality themselves. If this Joker feller hadn't sent out his rhymes and just behaved like a normal murderer, the general public wouldn't have been so quick to class him as a maniac.'

'Don't you think he's mad, then?'

'I'm just keepin' an open mind until

I've got somethin' more to go on. I've sufficient intelligence to realise that there may be more than one explanation, that's all.'

'But in this case — ' began Larry.

'This case isn't any different to any other case,' interrupted the superintendent. 'The only difference is that he selects people that don't appear to have any connection with each other, and before he kills 'em he sends 'em rhymes on a card bearin' a picture of a clown. Because we can't find any reason for his killin' 'em and sendin' his rhymes doesn't necessarily mean that there isn't one.'

'You always were an obstinate old devil,' said Larry rudely. 'Anyhow, I didn't come here to talk about crime, or to hear your views on the Joker. I've heard enough about him from Roone — '

'Who is this feller Roone you keep talkin' about?' grunted Mr. Budd, helping himself to another of his evil-smelling cigars.

'He's my neighbour,' explained Larry. 'He's a retired doctor. Nice chap. You'll probably meet him if you come down.'

The Rosebud raised his eyebrows. 'Come down? Where?'

'To my place. I want you to come back with me and see some roses I've grown for exhibition at the local flower show next week. They're beauties!'

Mr. Budd's habitual look of boredom vanished. 'There's nothing I'd like better, and there's no reason why I shouldn't take the afternoon off — '

'You've an appointment at six with the assistant commissioner,' ventured Sergeant Leek apologetically.

'That's the evenin', an' I can get back before then,' said Mr. Budd. 'Yes, I'll come, Mr. Weston. Perhaps lookin' at your roses'll give me some ideas. I solved the Ridgewell murders while I was at the Horticultural Hall.'

Larry Weston rose and stretched himself. 'I've got my car outside, and if we start now we shall get down to Dorking in time for lunch.'

The superintendent laboriously heaved himself out of his chair. 'That'll suit me,' he said, walking ponderously across the office and fetching his hat. He turned to the melancholy sergeant. 'If anythin' important comes in, you know where to find me an' you can phone. Mr. Weston's number is on my list.'

Leek nodded gloomily. 'Don't suppose I shall have to use it,' he muttered. 'There's nothing likely to be urgent.'

Larry's little two-seater was waiting in the square outside the entrance, and a few seconds later they joined the stream of traffic on the Embankment.

The friendship between these two had begun in a peculiar way. In the latter days of the war, Mr. Budd had been walking a beat as a uniformed constable. Captain Larry Weston, home on leave, had celebrated his penultimate evening too well. The Rosebud had found him in the small hours of the morning engaged in trying to fight an inoffensive taxi driver under the mistaken impression that that individual was the Kaiser. Reluctantly Mr. Budd at last marched him off to Marlborough Street, with the result that he spent an unpleasant night in a cold cell and woke in the morning a sadder and wiser man. After an unsympathetic magistrate had extracted a fine, Larry and the constable had gone to a small tea-shop near the police court where, under the influence of hot coffee, their acquaintance, started under such inauspicious conditions, had ripened into friendship. They discovered that there was one interest they possessed in common — an intense love of flowers, and for over two hours they discussed their mutual hobby.

After the war, Larry found himself out of the army and out of a job, with a rapidly dwindling gratuity. It was his friend the policeman who suggested he should set up as a landscape gardener. Larry had invested what was left of his gratuity in the rental of a small house on the outskirts of Dorking. Rather to his surprise, the business prospered from the first. There were quite a number of people who had made money out of the war, and these were only too pleased to commission Larry to design and lay out the grounds of their newly acquired estates to the best advantage.

In a few years Larry Weston was

well-established. He had tried hard in the early days to get his friend to leave the police force and join him as partner, but this Mr. Budd had steadfastly refused to do. He had been wise to do so, for ability, combined with a modicum of luck, had contributed to rapid promotion and inclusion in the coveted circle of the C.I.D. In eight years he passed from detective-constable through the intermediate stages to inspector, and eventually reached the rank of superintendent.

During the journey to Dorking, they talked roses with much enthusiasm and a wealth of technical detail.

'I've asked Roone to drop in this afternoon,' said Larry, skilfully steering the car between two buses. 'Flowers and crime are his hobby.'

'So long as he keeps off crime, I don't mind,' grunted the Rosebud. 'How long have you known him? You haven't mentioned him before.'

Larry slowed up before the outstretched hand of a traffic policeman. 'I only met him during the last six months. He's got a house about half a mile away from mine — I think I told you that. It was really through his secretary I got acquainted. She'd been down to the post office and twisted her ankle taking a short cut back across the fields. I happened to find her and took her home.'

'Oh, he's got a secretary, has he,' murmured Mr. Budd. 'What's she like?'

Out of the corner of his eye, the Rosebud saw Larry redden. 'Miss Grayson is — er — attractive.' He hastily changed the subject, and no further mention was made of the attractive Miss Grayson.

It was a little before one when they reached Larry's house, a low-roofed two-storied building that stood backed by trees in three and a half acres of ground. The trim well-shaven lawn and the masses of colour that blazed on all sides testified to its owner's work and hobby.

Mr. Budd got stiffly out of the car and looked about him with approval. 'Every time I come here,' he said with a sigh, 'I'm tempted to hand in my resignation. This is the kind of place I'd like when I retire. Somewhere where there isn't any crime except chicken stealing.'

'We're not quite as rural as that,' Larry laughed. 'There was a smash-and-grab raid in Dorking last week.'

He led the way inside, and they passed out of the sunlight into the cool shadows of the square hall. An elderly grey-haired woman came forward to meet them.

'I 'eard you arrive, sir.' She smiled. 'I expect you're 'ungry and would like your lunch at once, wouldn't you?'

'As soon as possible, please,' said Larry; and with a nod and a smile to the superintendent she disappeared through a door into the back of the house.

Mrs. Nadia Clipp and her husband constituted the entire staff of Larry's modest establishment. He had advertised for a married couple shortly after he had acquired the property, and out of the numerous applicants had chosen the Clipps. Mrs. Clipp cooked wonderfully well, and the house was kept spotless. Unfortunately, Mr. Alfred Clipp, an abstemious and sober man all the week, regularly got drunk on Sundays, and on these occasions he had to be put to bed by his wife. Larry had expostulated and threatened; Mrs. Clipp had pleaded and stormed; but all to no purpose.

'I can't 'elp it, sir,' the little man apologised dolefully after he had been harangued on this disgusting habit. ''Less I 'ave me drop of beer on a Sunday, I seems to go all to pieces-like for the rest of the week.'

His contrite wife had confirmed this statement. 'His father was just the same, sir,' she confided to Larry. 'Alf's an 'ard worker though, and a good 'usband, 'cept for his little failing. It ain't as if 'e was noisy when drunk; docile as a child 'e is. If you could overlook it, sir . . .'

Larry had decided to overlook it. Mr. Clipp's work did not suffer, and if he liked this form of recreation that was his own affair.

Mr. Budd remembered the eccentric behaviour of his host's servant as they went into the low-roofed dining-room, and enquired after him.

'Oh, yes, he's still the same every Sunday,' replied Larry. 'I don't bother about it now.'

'Funny how people get into habits,' remarked the Rosebud gently. 'I've got into a habit that I've never been able to break myself of. I always have a glass of beer just before lunch.'

Larry grinned.

'That's what makes you so fat,' he said, and went over to the sideboard.

3

Dr. Roone's Secretary

They lunched comfortably with the summer breeze blowing in through the open windows of the dining-room. When the meal was over and Mr. Budd had lighted one of his thin black cigars, Larry suggested they should go and see the rose garden.

The stout superintendent rose lazily and stretched himself. 'This is what I call life. A good lunch, a glass or two of real beer, and an afternoon in the garden. Makes you think catchin' criminals is an overrated pastime.'

Larry smiled as he conducted his visitor out into the little hall. Mr. Budd was fond of disparaging his profession, but the other knew that he loved it as much as he loved the hobby with which he passed his leisure hours.

Strolling across the strip of crazy

paving that bisected the lawn, they passed beneath a shady pergola into the rose garden. Mr. Budd paused at the top of the three steps that led down to it and gazed admiringly at the mass of colour before him. The light breeze carried the perfume of the blossoms to his nostrils. 'My idea of heaven,' he said.

Larry led him round, pointing out his choicest specimens and expatiating on the methods he had adopted to bring them to their present state of perfection.

'I've never seen better blooms,' Mr. Budd said. 'You ought to be certain of a 'first' with these.'

They discussed fertilisers and grafting, the blending of one standard with another, and the destruction of greenfly, and forgot the passing of time. The appearance of Mrs. Clipp at the head of the steps interrupted them, and Larry went over to see what she wanted.

'Dr. Roone and Miss Grayson have called, sir,' said the housekeeper. 'I've shown them into the drawing-room.'

'Bring them out here, and then get tea, will you?' said Larry, and with a smile and a nod the woman departed. Larry rejoined Mr. Budd.

'Roone's arrived,' he said, 'and he's brought Miss Grayson with him. I think you'll like him.'

'Not many people I don't like,' murmured the superintendent. ''Ceptin' criminals, the assistant commissioner, and occasionally bone-headed sergeants.'

Two figures appeared crossing the lawn, and Larry went to meet his visitors. Dr. Roone was a small rotund man with a round white face that was curiously flat, accounted for by the smallness of his nose. He had a ready laugh that displayed a set of very white and even teeth.

'What a glorious day, Mr. Weston,' he said as he shook hands with Larry. 'I've brought my secretary, Miss Grayson, with me. I hope you don't mind? She's tremendously keen on roses. Almost as keen as I am.'

Larry assured him that far from minding he was delighted, and Mr. Budd concluded from the expression on his face that this was no more than the truth. And after once glancing at the woman who had accompanied the doctor, he was not surprised. Norma Grayson was tall and slim, and in the simple summer frock she wore, she looked lovely. She had the flawless skin that sometimes goes with auburn hair, and her large violet-blue eyes were intelligent.

They surveyed Mr. Budd gravely when he was introduced. 'You are the first detective I've ever met,' she said with a smile.

Larry chuckled. 'Then you're getting full value, Miss Grayson,' he said, 'for there's enough of Budd to make three ordinary detectives.'

'Which only goes to show that I'm not an ordinary detective!' murmured the fat man good-humouredly.

By some accident or design — Mr. Budd was inclined to think it was the latter — he found himself paired with Doctor Roone.

'I've heard a lot about you, Superintendent,' said the doctor as they strolled round the rose garden in the wake of Larry and Norma. 'And I'm very pleased to have had this opportunity of making your acquaintance. I daresay Weston has told you that one of my hobbies is criminology.'

The Rosebud groaned inwardly. 'I believe he did mention somethin' of the sort. Look at those Drushkins — ain't they lovely?'

Roone stopped to admire the beautiful white blooms, but he was not to be put off. 'You're in charge of this Joker business, aren't you?' he said, and when Mr. Budd reluctantly admitted that he was: 'I'm terribly interested. I've followed the affair closely. What's the police theory?'

'The police seem to be the only people who haven't *got* a theory,' remarked Mr. Budd wearily. He had no wish to discuss crime with this jovial little man. The visit to Larry Weston's had offered a pleasant break from duty, and he was not inclined to spoil the promise of that lazy afternoon.

'It's my belief that these crimes are the work of a lunatic,' declared Dr. Roone with the air of a man making an original discovery.

Mr. Budd sighed. 'So say the entire press of this country, and my sergeant.'

Roone glanced at him quickly. 'But it's not your opinion, eh?'

'I haven't got an opinion,' replied the Rosebud, shaking his head. 'I'm one of those peculiar people who hate jumpin' to conclusions. When I've got him under lock and key, I'll be able to tell you!'

The doctor chuckled. 'Possibly I was indiscreet to try and probe into official secrets. My brother's always telling me that my curiosity will get me into serious trouble one of these days.' He changed the subject, and to the superintendent's relief began to expatiate on the peculiarities of his relative. His brother apparently lived in Paris and spent a great deal of his time travelling. He seldom came to England, but Dr. Roone was in the habit of paying him an occasional visit.

Mr. Budd was not particularly interested, but preferred this to a discussion on criminology and the Grim Joker. Larry and Norma Grayson had disappeared from sight, only to reappear when Mrs. Clipp came to announce that tea was waiting in the drawing-room.

Mr. Budd, tiring of the doctor's company, skilfully palmed him off onto Larry and attached himself to Norma as they strolled towards the house. She was full of admiration for Larry's roses.

'I don't think I've ever seen such fine specimens,' she said enthusiastically. 'Mr. Weston ought to be very proud of them.'

'You're fond of roses?' asked Mr. Budd.

'I think they're the most beautiful of all the flowers.' There was a warmth in her voice that bespoke sincerity. She was not being conventionally polite, or just making conversation.

'I've got a lot of roses in my little patch of garden,' he said. 'Of course, they're not as good as Larry's. I don't get the time to spend on 'em. But they're pretty good for an amateur.'

He became eloquent on his favourite topic, and Norma glanced at him curiously.

'You're thinkin' rose growin' is a funny hobby for a detective?' He smiled, and she reddened slightly.

'I *was* thinking something of the sort,' she admitted.

'A lot of people have thought the same. But there's a great deal in common between my profession and my hobby.'

She looked puzzled.

'Roses are difficult to grow because so many parasites attack 'em,' Mr. Budd explained. 'And life's difficult for the same reason. Criminals and greenfly are both parasites, and neither roses nor civilisation can flourish if they're allowed to get the upper hand.'

Before she could comment on this remark, they had reached the house and Dr. Roone and Larry had joined them.

Tea in the big cool drawing-room was very pleasant. Norma presided, and Mr. Budd, comfortably ensconced in a deep armchair, thought the room made an effective background for the slim woman as she bent over the tea things.

Larry evidently thought the same, for although he was listening to Dr. Roone's chatter, his eyes were watching Norma's every movement. Mr. Budd guessed that Larry's bachelor days were in danger of drawing to a close. Well, she was a nice woman, and she liked roses. The Clipps were all very well, but the house needed a mistress to look after it properly.

Mr. Budd took the cup of tea Norma held out to him and dropped in three lumps of sugar, stirring it thoughtfully.

'By the way,' said Dr. Roone, 'that little cottage near my place is let.'

'You mean Whitegate?' asked Larry.

The doctor nodded. 'Yes. I don't know who's got the place, but I saw a lot of furniture going in this morning.'

Mr. Budd, whose thoughts were still centred on Norma, saw her change colour. Her hands, which had been deftly using the cake knife, faltered, and she nearly dropped it. Neither of the other two noticed her agitation, and the superintendent wondered as to its cause.

Whatever it was, Norma quickly recovered. 'I think the place has been taken by an invalid,' she said smoothly. 'At least, that's what Mrs. Hewitt at the post office told me.'

'Then you can take it that it has,' Dr. Roone said. 'There's nothing happens round here that Mrs. Hewitt doesn't know. That woman ought to have been a reporter. Her curiosity is insatiable.'

The conversation drifted into other channels, and presently the doctor announced that they must be going. He shook hands heartily with Mr. Budd, and Larry escorted his guests to the door.

When he came back, Mr. Budd was standing gazing out of the window, puffing slowly at a freshly lighted cigar. 'I'll have to be goin' too, Larry. I've got a conference at six.'

'I'll drive you back,' said his friend. 'What do you think of Roone and Miss Grayson?'

'He seems a cheery fellow,' said the Rosebud carefully. 'Bit borin', but not as bad as some I've met. I had a job to keep him off crime.'

Larry chuckled. 'I thought you would,' he said. 'Isn't she a charming woman?'

'Very charmin',' agreed Mr. Budd. 'What's this feller Roone want a secretary for?'

'I don't know,' Larry said.

'Hm! Well, I don't suppose he'll keep this one very long.'

'Why?' Larry demanded, astonished. 'Did she say she was leaving?'

'She didn't say so,' murmured Mr. Budd, 'and I don't think she knows she is. But her next job won't be as a secretary.'

He smiled as he looked at his friend, and catching his meaning Larry flushed. 'Why, I've only seen her three times. You're a matchmaking old woman, Budd!'

Mr. Budd sighed wearily. 'When I see a young feller gapin' at a pretty woman like you was gapin' at Miss Grayson, I naturally form my own conclusions. An' I'll bet they're right, too.'

Late that night as he drove back in his dilapidated little car to his unpretentious Streatham villa, Mr. Budd recalled the afternoon at Dorking, and one of the things that stood out most clearly in his memory was Norma's agitation at her employer's apparently innocent remark that the cottage near his house had been let. He pondered over it as he ate the supper which his housekeeper had prepared for him.

It was not until two weeks later that he found an answer, and by that time so many things had happened that the reason for Norma Grayson's momentary perturbation seemed almost insignificant in comparison.

4

Mr. Kyne Transacts His Business

Halfway down New Bond Street there was a side turning in which stood a large block of modern and imposing flats, the last word in expensiveness, if not in comfort. Polished doors of rosewood admitted you to the vestibule, a place of soft lights and costly woods and thick pile carpets into which the feet would sink as into an old and well-kept lawn. There was an automatic lift with gilded doors for the convenience of the residents, and, in a little glass office under the carved stairway, a discreet porter in a sombre uniform. A tactful and obliging man, always ready for such services as come within the limits of his duty.

On the fourth floor of this impressive edifice, Mr. Oswald Kyne occupied a large and luxuriously furnished flat. It was generally supposed by the other residents, when they thought about him at all, that Mr. Kyne was a retired businessman. That he was rich followed as a natural consequence. The fact that he lived in a suite in such an expensive building as Rochester House, and possessed a polished and glittering Rolls of the latest model to take him back and forth when he went out, was sufficient testimony to his wealth.

To a certain extent they were right. Mr. Kyne was both rich and a businessman, but he had by no means retired. From his comfortable if rather ornate study he still conducted such business as came to his hand, and found it very profitable indeed. Neither was it known that Rochester House belonged to Mr. Kyne, for he was, apparently, a shy man and concealed his ownership behind the Rochester Estate Company Ltd., to whom the other tenants' cheques for rent were made payable.

That Mr. Kyne was extremely particular regarding the people who occupied his flats was evinced by the extraordinary care which the Rochester Estate Company Ltd. took in selecting their tenants.

Only those people with the highest references were considered as suitable to occupy the same building as Mr. Kyne. To live at Rochester House was the hallmark of ultra-respectability.

Mr. Kyne himself lived a very retiring life. He seldom entertained, and only occasionally visited the theatre. Punctually at half-past seven every night, his car with its neat chauffeur would glide up to the entrance of Rochester House. Mr. Kyne would descend in the lift, remark upon the state of the weather to the deferential porter, and be driven off to one of the more sober restaurants, where he would eat a carefully chosen dinner. At nine o'clock precisely, except on those occasions when he went on to a play, his car would deposit him at Rochester House, and he would ascend to his flat and not be seen again that night.

He was fond of good wines, but drank sparingly, and altogether lived an exemplary life.

On a warm summer afternoon when the streets were thronged with coolly clad sauntering figures, a tall smartly dressed man in grey came slowly down New Bond Street and turned into the narrow thoroughfare containing Rochester House. Entering the vestibule, he stepped into the waiting automatic lift with an assured air, pressed the button and was carried noiselessly up to the fourth floor. Leaving the lift, he crossed the carpeted corridor and, pausing outside the polished door of Mr. Kyne's flat, raised his hand and gave a gentle and peculiar tap on the small grotesquely patterned bronze knocker.

'Is he in?' he asked, smiling pleasantly at the neatly dressed maid who opened the door.

'I don't know. I'll see.' Her hard face remained expressionless except for the habitual scowl that marred the smoothness of her brow. The visitor took no notice of her ungraciousness, but stepped across the threshold into the square and beautifully furnished hall.

The scowling servant shut the door and went across to another on the left. Without knocking, she opened it and disappeared into the room beyond. After a moment or two, she came back. 'Mr. Kyne will see you,' she said curtly.

He crossed over to the room from which she had just emerged, and she held the door open for him to enter. He found himself in a large and luxuriously furnished apartment that was half study, half office. The walls were panelled with polished walnut, and the chairs and lounges upholstered in costly brocade. At a rather ornate Empire writing table, a man was seated, scanning a legal-looking document he laid aside as the visitor entered, and raised his head.

'Good afternoon, Slade. I expected you,' he said briefly, and waved a fat hand towards a chair facing him.

Mr. Oswald Kyne was a smooth man in every sense of the word. Smooth was his thin, greying hair, brushed back from his high forehead. Smooth were his plump white hands, glittering with too many rings; and smooth was his heavy jowled, clean-shaven face. 'Oily' would perhaps have described him better, but the expression would have shocked Mr. Kyne's sensitive nature. He was a money-lender by profession, a fence and blackmailer by inclination; and because nature had supplied him with a criminal brain, Mr. Kyne had only one illusion left in the world — that he was a gentleman.

'Sit down,' he said in a deep rolling voice that sounded as if he mentally smacked his lips at every word. 'What have you brought me?'

The newcomer slipped a well-manicured hand into his breast pocket and withdrew a small package. Unfastening it, he disclosed a glittering string of emeralds.

'They're worth fifty thousand pounds,' he said, pushing them across the desk towards the other.

Mr. Kyne picked them up and examined them carefully. 'Not to me,' he said, shaking his head. 'They're too well-known. They couldn't be got rid of without being cut up, and that'd destroy most of their value.'

'Even then they'd be worth a good deal,' said the visitor.

Mr. Kyne frowned, turning the glittering string this way and that in his fat fingers. 'I'll give you a thousand for them,' he said at length.

'I should think you would,' grunted Slade. 'What do you think I am, a mug? I'm not parting with 'em under five thousand, and that's definite!'

Mr. Kyne shrugged his shoulders and threw the necklace back across the desk. 'Then we don't deal.'

'Why not? You can make a good profit at that price — '

'Never mind how much profit I'd make,' said Mr. Kyne impatiently. 'I've told you what I'm prepared to pay, and if you don't like to accept it, that's your business.'

'A thousand's a pretty low figure,' grumbled the other.

'You can take it or leave it,' said the smooth man indifferently.

'Make it two thousand.'

Mr. Kyne shook his head and smiled. 'A thousand or nothing,' he said decisively, 'and I'm telling you, Slade, that I'd rather it was nothing. I'm not keen on buying those stones; I'll have a lot of trouble in disposing of 'em. Everybody knows the Dyson Emeralds. If you don't want to sell at that price, take 'em somewhere else.'

The dark-featured Slade hesitated. 'Make it fifteen hundred for luck?' he suggested.

'Whose luck? Yours? No, we're wasting time. Put 'em away, my friend. I don't want 'em.'

Slade stretched out his hand, picked up the necklace and began slowly to repack it. Mr. Kyne watched him, a twinkle of amusement in his eyes. 'All right,' said Slade suddenly. 'I'll take your thousand.'

The man behind the desk, who had been certain that he would accept the offer from the beginning, rose to his feet, went over to a panel in the wall, and sliding it to one side, disclosed the polished steel door of a safe. Taking a key from his pocket, he unlocked it, withdrew a packet of notes, skinned several from the wad and, replacing the remainder, shut and locked the safe and pushed the panel back into place. 'There you are,' he said, coming over to the desk and throwing the notes in front of his visitor.

'And you've been well paid.'

'Well paid!' grumbled Slade as he counted them carefully. 'I like that. You've got the best of the bargain — you always do.'

'Then why come to me?' said Mr. Kyne, taking the emeralds and slipping them into his pocket. 'I'll tell you why. You come to me because I'm safe, and you've got to pay for safety, my friend.'

The hotel thief rose to his feet. 'You'll get copped one day, Kyne,' he said. 'You've been lucky up to now, but your luck won't last forever.'

'I shan't live forever,' said Mr. Kyne genially. 'Good afternoon, Slade, an' I'll be happy to see anythin' else that may — er — come into your possession.'

The man took his departure grumblingly, and when he had gone Mr. Kyne went over to the radiator that warmed his apartment. Pressing an innocent-looking nut, he uncovered a cavity in the dummy portion of the radiator, and into this he dropped the emeralds he had just bought.

Returning to his desk, he sat down, a complacent smile on his face. The afternoon had been a profitable one, and the evening was likely to prove even more profitable.

He took a cigar from a silver box in front of him, carefully pierced the end, and lighting it, lay back in his chair smoking thoughtfully.

Mr. Oswald Kyne had many irons in the fire, and the majority of them brought him a handsome revenue. That evening he was thinking of adding to their number — and in this he made the greatest mistake of his life, for he was not only to get severely burnt, but eventually lose his life in pitting his brain against a man infinitely cleverer than he, and much more dangerous.

5

The Telephone Message

Mr. Budd spent six busy — and so far as results were concerned, unproductive — days following his afternoon at Larry Weston's.

His interview with the assistant commissioner had been a little strained. They disliked each other at the best of times. Mr. Budd's methods were sometimes unconventional, and displeased the routine-loving Colonel Royce. On these occasions he was wont to send for the stout man and give tongue to his displeasure in no uncertain manner. Mr. Budd would listen to these admonishments without comment and end up, to the exasperation of the assistant commissioner, by agreeing with him.

'But I've got me own way of workin', sir,' he would conclude, 'an' I can't work any other way. It's just a matter of temperament.'

Since in nine cases out of ten he proved that his way was the right one, Colonel Royce nearly always found himself at a disadvantage. The advent of the Grim Joker and Mr. Budd's complete failure to discover anything about that elusive person had, however, given the assistant commissioner an excuse for being a little more unpleasant than usual.

He had said a lot of things he had been wanting to say for many months, and although the stout man had listened in his usual sleepy manner, he had left the office with tightened lips and his florid face a little redder than usual. That there was some justification for Colonel Royce's irritability he was the first to admit. Up to the present he had fallen down badly on the case. It was now nearly six months since the unfortunate Hamilton Lorne had been found dead in his bed, and Mr. Budd was no nearer the discovery of his murderer than he had been then.

He had done everything that was humanly possible, but at Scotland Yard they judged by results, and his results had been nil.

Over and over again he read through the accounts of the three crimes, hoping to stumble on something that would give him a new line, but he found nothing. Neither did the countless enquiries he instituted yield any fresh information. The three murders perpetrated by the humorous assassin looked like joining the ranks of the few undiscovered crimes that smirched the record of Scotland Yard.

It was a weary and harassed man who ascended the stone staircase to his office on the morning of the sixth day and was greeted by the lugubrious Sergeant Leek. 'Anythin' come in?' asked Mr. Budd as he sank into the chair behind his desk.

The thin sergeant shook his head. 'Nothing you'd call important,' he answered. 'There's a report in about that raid last night on Hammond's spelling house, and they sent down from upstairs asking for a report on the Lime Street business.'

Mr. Budd growled something uncomplimentary about the people upstairs and the Lime Street business, glowered at the typewritten report on the Knightsbridge gaming house, pushed it aside impatiently, and leaned back in his chair with knitted brows.

Leek sighed resignedly and subsided into a chair. Mr. Budd was apt to be a little difficult when he was worried, and perhaps the weather had something to do with it too. It was a grey, cloudy and oppressive morning. The sergeant turned his mournful eyes towards the window. It looked as though there was a storm brewing. The sky had a tinge of copper about it.

Quite unconsciously, Leek's drooping lips pursed themselves and he began softly to whistle a tuneless dirge. After two minutes of this, Mr. Budd's huge bulk moved restlessly and his closed eyes opened.

'Must you do that?' he asked wearily. 'If you must have music, we'll get a gramophone. Or maybe you'd prefer a barrel organ?'

The unfortunate sergeant looked at the moment as if he would prefer the power of becoming invisible.

'I don't expect you to be of any assistance,' went on the stout man witheringly, 'but at least you can keep quiet!' He closed his eyes again and settled himself more comfortably in his chair. A deathly hush filled the office, accentuated rather than dispelled by the traffic sounds from the Embankment.

Mr. Budd appeared to have fallen asleep. His hands were clasped across his capacious stomach, and his chins had sunk onto his chest. Appearances were deceptive, however, for his brain had never been more alert. Once again he was going over all that was known of the Grim Joker, trying to find a fresh starting point for further investigations, and he couldn't find anything of the sort. If the limerick-man committed no further crime, there was every possibility that he would never be caught. Mr. Budd's greatest hope was that one of his grotesque warnings would be received by some fresh person marked out as an intended victim. He had been hoping this for a long time, but as the days passed and nothing happened he became less and less optimistic. It looked as if the killing of the unfortunate Miss Rothe had been his last 'joke'.

The sudden ringing of the telephone bell broke the silence of the room, and Sergeant Leek half-rose to reach for the instrument, but Mr. Budd's hand had already closed round the receiver. Jerking himself to a sitting position, he rested his large elbow on the desk and put the receiver to his ear.

'Hello!' he growled. 'Yes. Superintendent Budd speakin'.'

There was a long pause while he listened to someone at the other end of the wire. Leek, watching, saw his face change. His lips pressed together and his eyes narrowed, sure signs that the stout man was unusually interested.

'When did it arrive?' he asked; and then, after a short interval: 'All right, I'll come down at once. In the meanwhile, don't leave the house under any pretext whatever, and keep someone you can trust with you until I arrive.'

He hung up the black cylinder and

looked across the desk at the interested Leek. 'That message was from Dr. Roone,' he said grimly. 'The Grim Joker's turned up again. He received a card by this mornin's post, and accordin' to the usual rhyme on the back, the time of his death has been fixed for twelve o'clock — midday!'

6

The Man Who Laughed

A jagged ribbon of blue light flickered across the horizon to the south and was followed a few seconds later by a reverberating crash of thunder. The police driver glanced anxiously at the lowering black storm clouds that had so swiftly piled themselves up in the sky, and pressed his foot a little harder on the accelerator.

'I think we can just about make it, sir,' he murmured to Mr. Budd, and the stout man grunted.

'How much further have we to go?' asked Leek, clutching desperately at his hat as an unexpected burst of wind came sweeping across the open country and threatened to tear it from his head.

'About five miles, maybe a trifle less,' replied Mr. Budd, his half-closed eyes on the road ahead. 'Roone lives just on the other side of Dorkin'.'

A second peal of thunder, louder than the first, drowned the end of the sentence, and a large spot of rain splashed the windscreen, followed by another and another. The storm that had threatened when they had left the Yard in the big open police car had burst. As a matter of fact they must have run into it, for the rain was pelting down, and the rolling roar of the thunder was almost incessant, as with the screen-wiper working madly they tore through the narrow streets of Dorking.

It may have been due to the storm, or perhaps to an unusual sixth sense, but the Rosebud felt a sudden fit of depression steal over him when, leaving the old town behind them, they once more came out on the open high road. It was as though a gigantic hand had attached a heavy weight to his heart, and try as he would, he could not shake off the unpleasant feeling.

The shining surface of the road rendered driving difficult, and the big car slithered and skidded as the man at the wheel sent it forward at the utmost speed he dared. They were running now between straggling hedges, each leaf a miniature cataract behind which lay dripping fields of vegetables and bedraggled corn, lit up clearly every few seconds by the almost continuous flicker of the lightning.

Passing a plantation of wheat in the middle of which stood a melancholy and forlorn-looking scarecrow, its tattered rain-soaked garments flapping dismally in the gusts of wind, they presently came to the red-brick pillars giving entrance to a drive.

'Here we are,' grunted Mr. Budd as the driver skilfully swung the car into the broad gravel way that lay beyond. 'This is the place.'

'Just the sort of day that feller *would* choose,' grumbled Leek as the big man pressed the polished brass bell at the side of the door, and, removing his hat, shook it vigorously.

They waited, and after a slight interval the double doors were opened noiselessly by a black-clad servant, obviously the butler.

'Your master is expectin' us,' said Mr. Budd. 'I'm Superintendent Budd. Will you tell him I've arrived?'

The butler, a stout, sleek-looking individual with jet-black hair immaculately plastered down on either side of a central parting, regarded him with a look of puzzled astonishment. 'Dr. Roone certainly *was* expecting you, sir,' he said civilly, but markedly stressing the 'was'. 'I understood, however, that he'd gone to Dorking to meet you.'

'Do you mean he's out?' asked the Rosebud, his eyes narrowing.

'Yes, sir,' replied the man, and the expression on his face was even more puzzled. 'He went out about half an hour ago — directly after you telephoned.'

'I never telephoned at all!' snapped Mr. Budd, and the sense of foreboding that he had experienced before increased.

'Didn't you, sir? I don't quite understand. There must be some mistake. Perhaps you'd better see Dr. Roone's secretary; she took the message.'

'I think I had,' murmured Mr. Budd

57

grimly, and he stepped into the comfortably furnished hall as the butler stood aside.

'Will you come this way?' invited the man, closing the door and leading them across the polished floor to a tiny smoking-room on the left. Having ushered them in, he bowed and withdrew.

As soon as they were alone, the Rosebud turned to Leek with a troubled look on his face that he made no attempt to conceal. 'I don't like it,' he said, shaking his head. 'I certainly sent no telephone message, as you know, and it looks to me as if this Joker feller got to hear we were comin' and lured Roone out with a false call. If that's the case — '

He stopped abruptly, and going over to the window stared out with unseeing eyes at a mass of rain-soaked shrubbery. But his silence was more ominous than if he had completed the sentence.

Leek felt a little shiver creep up his spine, and it was not due to his wet clothing. 'Twelve o'clock was the time, wasn't it?' he whispered hoarsely.

'That's what Roone said,' replied Mr. Budd, and glanced at his watch. 'It's barely eleven yet, so — '

The sound of a light step outside made him pause, and a moment later the door opened and Norma Grayson entered. There was a worried look on her face as she greeted the stout man.

'Will you come into the library, Mr. Budd?' she said. 'It's more comfortable there.'

The superintendent nodded, and she led the way out in the hall and up the broad staircase, talking as she went.

'I can't make out how there could have been any misunderstanding,' she said, opening a door on the first landing and admitting them into a large book-lined room furnished heavily but comfortably with deep leather-covered chairs and lounges, 'for I myself took the telephone message calling Dr. Roone out.'

'Did the caller say he was me?' enquired Mr. Budd, warming himself in front of a glowing electric radiator.

'Yes,' she answered, 'otherwise the doctor would not have gone out. The voice was like yours, too,' she added doubtfully.

'Well, I can assure you I sent no message,' declared the superintendent. 'What did this fellow say?'

'It sounded quite plausible to me,' she answered, 'and neither Dr. Roone nor I suspected for a moment that it didn't come from you. The man who telephoned and gave your name said that you'd got as far as Dorking but couldn't get any further owing to a puncture. He said you'd put the car in the garage of the White Hart Hotel, and would Dr. Roone meet you there immediately, as the storm was so bad. I asked the doctor what I should say, and he replied: 'Tell the superintendent I'll leave at once'.'

Mr. Budd's heart sank and he rubbed the side of his face irritably. The cleverness of the thing lay in its very simplicity — it was just what might so easily have happened. 'And that was all?' he asked.

'No, there was one other thing,' she said, and for the first time her cool, level voice shook slightly. 'The man who rang up particularly requested that Dr. Roone should bring with him the card he had received this morning.'

'And of course he took it,' said Mr. Budd. 'Tell me, Miss Grayson, did the doctor leave here on foot?'

'No, he went in his car.'

'Alone?'

'Yes, he always drove himself — a small two seater coupé.' And then as she noticed his frown deepen: 'Do you think anything can have happened to him? He told me about the card and — '

'I'm very much afraid the worst has happened,' answered Mr. Budd, and Leek had never heard his voice so troubled. 'There's just a chance that the car may have saved him. The Joker may not have been prepared for a car.' He thought quickly. 'Is there any other means of gettin' from here to Dorkin' except by the main road?'

Norma shook her head.

'Then he certainly never went there, or we should have passed him, and we passed nothin'.'

'Perhaps,' she said hopefully, 'he

reached the White Hart before you got to the town.'

'There's just a possibility he may have,' agreed Mr. Budd, but his tone was doubtful. 'However, we can soon see. Would you mind ringin' up the White Hart and askin' if Dr. Roone has been there, Miss Grayson?'

She went over to the instrument, which stood on a large roll-top desk in the centre of the room, and, consulting a directory, gave a number and was put through.

After a few seconds she turned from the telephone. 'They've seen nothing of Dr. Roone at the White Hart,' she announced in a low voice that trembled in spite of her efforts to keep it steady.

The Rosebud nodded several times, but his face was expressionless. 'I never expected they would. Somewhere between here and Dorkin' the Grim Joker was waitin' for him, and he's got him!' His mouth set, and suddenly his sleepy eyes opened very wide. Surprisingly active, he strode over to the door. 'Come on, Leek,' he said with his hand on the knob, 'we've got to find

Dr. Roone. I'm afraid we're too late to save him, but we've got to find him — alive or otherwise.'

He had the door half-open when the telephone bell whirred persistently. The sound was so unexpected that Norma jumped, a testimony to her strained nerves, and turned to the instrument. 'Perhaps this is Dr. Roone,' she suggested as she picked up the receiver, but Mr. Budd knew she only said it as a forlorn hope; knew that she would be surprised if she were right.

'Yes?' she called into the vulcanite mouthpiece. 'Yes, this is the Larches.'

A pause followed, and the stout man saw a peculiar expression cross her face — an expression in which wonder and fear were curiously mingled.

'Yes, he's here now,' she continued, still with that odd look on her face. 'Who is it speaking?' Again there was a pause while she listened to the reply, and then: 'Very well, I'll tell him,' she said, and glancing up at the detective who was standing by her side, held out the receiver. 'Someone wants to speak to you, Mr. Budd. A man.

He wouldn't give his name.'

With a sudden unaccountable quickening of his pulse, the Rosebud placed the black cylinder to his ear. 'Who is it?' he asked.

Over the wire floated a little babbling laugh. 'That Superintendent Budd?' enquired a high, squeaky voice. 'Thought I might catch you. He-he-he, even if you can't catch me. He-he-he!'

The stolid superintendent felt his flesh creep as he heard the little trilling peals of laughter that interspersed the staccato sentences. There was something horrible and sinister about that inane chuckling.

'I had to ring you up,' the toneless voice continued. 'Too good a joke to keep all to myself. He-he-he. Do you want to laugh, Budd, eh? If you do, go and look for Roone. He-he-he.'

'Who are you?' demanded Mr. Budd as the other broke off to laugh breathlessly.

'Wouldn't you like to know?' came the reply. 'But you never will. He-he-he! That's what makes it all so amusing. Go and look for Roone, Budd. He-he-he! You'll laugh till you cry when you find him. He looks so funny!'

There was a final chuckle and a click as the unknown rang off.

7

Not At All Funny

'Who was it?' asked Norma with a shiver, white to the lips. She had been standing close enough to hear that high-pitched inane laugh.

'The Grim Joker,' answered Mr. Budd, his fingers grasping at the hook of the telephone.

Sergeant Leek gave a gasp. 'What was he ringin' up for?'

His question fell on deaf ears, for the superintendent was already talking to the exchange. 'Hello!' he called. 'That call that came through just now. Will you tell me where it originated? Yes, I know all about your rules, but this is police business. Be quick please!' He waited impatiently, his fingers drumming on the top of the desk.

An age seemed to pass — in reality it was less than a minute — before Mr.

Budd got his answer. 'Your call came from a public box in the post office, High Street, Dorking,' said the emotionless voice of the telephone operator.

The Rosebud grunted a word of thanks and hung up the receiver. Turning to the gaping sergeant and Norma, he gave them the gist of the unknown's message. 'Dr. Roone's somewhere in the vicinity of this house,' he concluded. 'I'm sure of that. And the first thing we've got to do is to find him. I should say he's at some point between here and Dorkin' — or rather, his body is,' he added bitterly. 'We were too late to save him. The only thing we can hope for now is that we shall discover some clue that'll lead us to his murderer.'

As he finished speaking there came a knock on the door, and the sleek butler appeared. 'Mr. Weston has called, Miss, to see Dr. Roone,' he said.

Norma uttered an exclamation. 'Show him into the drawing-room — ' she began, but Mr. Budd interrupted her.

'I'd like to see Larry,' he said. 'D'you think he could come up here?'

'Of course,' she answered. 'Bring Mr. Weston up here, Sellick.'

The butler gave them a curious glance and withdrew, and a few minutes later ushered Larry into the room.

'I hope I'm not dis — ' he began, stopping as he caught sight of Mr. Budd. 'Hello, Budd! What on earth are you doing here?'

The stout man told him, and Larry's face went grave. 'My God! Surely it can't be as bad as you think?'

'I hope it isn't,' said Mr. Budd. 'It certainly couldn't be worse than I think. Perhaps you'd like to come with us and help with the search. You know the neighbourhood better than I do.'

'Of course I'll come with you,' said Larry, looking anxiously at Norma. 'This is dreadful for you, Miss Grayson.'

'It's worse for Dr. Roone,' broke in the Rosebud, 'so don't let's waste any more time.'

'You — you'll let me know if you find anything, won't you?' said Norma.

'Of course we will,' answered Larry. 'We'll come back here in any case.' He gave her a reassuring smile and followed Mr. Budd and the thin sergeant down the stairs.

The storm had passed over, although there was a faint muttering of thunder in the distance, but the rain was still falling heavily. Except for mechanically turning up the collar of his coat, Mr. Budd seemed unconscious of this as he got into the car beside the driver and gave him a brief order.

'Where do we go first?' said Larry as the car shot forward with a jerk.

'We're going slowly along the road in the direction of the town, the way we came,' answered Mr. Budd. 'And we're goin' to keep a sharp lookout for any traces of Roone or his car, or both. If you and Leek take the left-hand side of the road, I'll take the right.'

There was no need to look far, as it happened, for as they turned out of the drive Larry gave a sharp exclamation and pointed ahead. 'Look! There, Budd!' he cried excitedly, leaning forward and gripping the stout man's shoulder. Close to the plantation of wheat, its bonnet half-buried in the ditch at the side of the road, was a small two-seater coupé.

'That wasn't there when we arrived,' said Leek, breathing hard. 'Must have been put there while we were actually in the house.'

'Say somethin' that isn't obvious!' growled the Rosebud, and he waited until they drew abreast of the small car and came to a halt.

Getting down, he stood for a moment gazing at the wet, slushy surface of the road. The tracks of the two-seater were plainly visible, for apparently no other traffic had passed that way since it had been ditched, and he could see the high ridges of mud that the wheels had thrown up when it had swerved suddenly. With a word of warning to the others not to obliterate the marks, he walked a few yards back the way they had come, and presently stopped, bending slightly forward.

The wheel tracks at this point were appreciably deeper, and between them was a tiny pool of black oil. 'Here's the place where he was held up,' he said, pointing this out to Larry and the sergeant. 'It's obvious that the car stopped here for several minutes.'

The young man nodded. 'The Grim Joker must have moved pretty quickly,' he said. 'Allowing that it took a quarter of an hour after the bogus telephone message for Roone to get out his car and reach this spot, I don't see how he could have got here from Dorking in the time.'

'He couldn't,' said Mr. Budd, 'unless he's got wings. Even in a car he couldn't do it with the roads in this state, and there are no signs of any other car havin' been here, except our own.'

'Then he must have had an accomplice who did the phoning,' said Larry.

'If that call came from Dorkin', yes,' agreed the Rosebud with a wrinkled brow. 'But we've no evidence that it did.'

'There isn't another call box nearer,' said Larry. 'And he must have used a call office, unless — '

'Unless he used a private phone,' broke in Mr. Budd, 'which means that he must live somewhere in the immediate neighbourhood. That's worth thinkin' about.'

'You could easily put it to the test,' said Larry excitedly. 'It shouldn't be difficult to find out from the exchange where that first phone call came from.'

'Maybe.' Mr. Budd pursed his lips and scratched the side of his face. 'He'd have realised that, though, so I'm afraid that even if we did trace the call it would only lead to a dead end. There's no harm in tryin' when we get back to the house. In the meanwhile, we'd better have a look at that car.'

He turned and walked back to the capsized coupé. It lay half on the path and half in the broad ditch that bordered the road, reared up at a drunken angle. Wondering what horror he was going to find, Mr. Budd pulled open the door and looked inside.

It was with a little shock of surprise that he saw it was empty, for he had expected to find the body of Roone. There were ample traces of a tragedy having taken place there, however, for the light upholstery of the seat was dappled with great splashes of blood that glistened in the light from the door; and when the detective touched one of these with his finger he found it was still wet.

'Good God, it's like a slaughterhouse!' exclaimed Larry, peering in over his shoulder.

'That's a very good description,' murmured Mr. Budd, 'for undoubtedly that's the use to which it's been put. The question is, where's the body?' He straightened up and looked about him, but there was no sign of the missing doctor, either dead or alive. The frown between his eyes deepened. Had the Grim Joker carried off the body of his unfortunate victim — and if so, for what conceivable purpose?

Mr. Budd had no doubt whatever now that Roone was dead. No man could have been wounded sufficiently to have caused all that blood and still remain alive. Besides, that jeering message from the unknown murderer was enough proof. He would never have phoned unless he had carried out his threat. But why hadn't he left the body in the car? The stout man shook his head in answer to his own unspoken question, and then swung round sharply as Sergeant Leek's voice called out to him.

The sergeant had been searching round the derelict coupé and was now standing on the other side of the ditch, pointing to a ragged break in the hedge that divided the wheat field from the road. 'Somebody's been through here,' he called. 'The wheat's all trampled down and there's more blood.'

Mr. Budd scrambled heavily across the ditch and joined him, Larry following. The field was a morass of half-liquid mud into which he sank up to his ankles, but he was too interested in the sergeant's discovery to pay it any heed. The wheat was crushed and broken as though by the passage of some heavy object, and the green of it stained here and there an ugly red — sinister marks that left little room for doubt as to what it was that had been dragged across that place.

'There's no doubt he came this way,' murmured the Rosebud, a little puzzled. 'But why did he bother to take so much trouble? I can't understand . . . ' Raising his eyes and looking ahead, he suddenly realised the reason for the Grim Joker's action, and there came to his mind one sentence spoken in that high-pitched, squeaky voice: '*He looks so funny.*'

'God in Heaven!' he cried, and there was a note of horror in his voice. 'The scarecrow!'

Careless of the mud that splashed him from head to foot, he went lumbering in the direction of the forlorn, bedraggled dummy that he knew was not a dummy but a lifeless thing that had once been a living, breathing man . . .

There it was, the supreme joke of this perverted joker, hanging limply from the supports that had formed the framework of the original — a horrible, faceless travesty of a human being that made even the hardened Leek go white as he looked at it.

Pinned to the tattered coat was a stained and crumpled card, and the grinning figure of the gaily garbed fool seemed to be pointing mockingly at Mr. Budd as he detached the sodden pasteboard and read the doggerel verse scrawled on the other side:

I don't like your face, Dr. Roone.
It is white, round, and flat, like a
  moon.
It annoys me to know
That you're living, and so
I shall take steps to kill you — by
  noon.

Silently, for he felt momentarily bereft of words, the stout man handed the card to Larry, and as he did so a church clock somewhere in the vicinity chimed the hour of twelve.

8

The Listener

'It's horrible!' whispered Larry huskily. 'Horrible, Budd! I experienced some ghastly things during the war, but nothing equal to this.'

Mr. Budd, his big face stern and set, bent over the body that they had succeeded in cutting loose from the frame of the scarecrow. 'The man who did this must be a devil!' he muttered, gently covering the head with his handkerchief. 'Except for the clothes and the contents of the pockets, I don't think anybody would be able to recognise it.'

'I can understand murder up to a point,' remarked Larry with a shiver. 'Given no conscience and a distorted sense of values, anybody might become a murderer — but this is sheer wanton brutality!'

'It certainly looks like it,' murmured

the Rosebud, busily examining a little pile of odds and ends that he had removed from the dead man's pockets and placed on a second handkerchief borrowed from Larry for the purpose. 'And yet, I don't know . . . somethin' seems to tell me that there's a purpose behind it all. And a pretty strong purpose, too.'

'I believe the feller's a lunatic,' said Leek. 'I've said so from the beginning. He's stark raving mad. That's why we can't catch him. Because there's no motive.'

'I agree with you,' said Larry. 'Nobody but a maniac could do a thing like this.'

'One of the sanest men I ever knew,' murmured Mr. Budd absently as he searched through the contents of a leather wallet that had been in the pockets of the dead man's clothing, 'cut up his wife into small pieces and buried her in the back garden. They tried to make out he was mad at the trial, but the doctors certified that he was as sane as the judge.'

'But he only committed one murder,' said Larry, 'and this is the Grim Joker's fourth. What's that you've found?'

The Rosebud was staring with rapt attention at a five-pound note he had taken from the pocketbook. 'Only a banknote,' he replied. 'But it's rather curious.'

'Why?' asked Larry. 'Roone was quite well off. I don't see anything curious in his having a five-pound note on him.'

'So far as that goes, neither do I,' said Mr. Budd. 'But when I find 'Julia Rothe, Rose Cottage, Horsham', written on the back, I'm entitled to think it's curious.'

'What?' Larry almost shouted the word, and stumbling over to the stout man's side bent down and saw the faint pencil writing. 'What do you make of it?'

'Nothin',' answered the superintendent, 'except that it's a very extraordinary thing. Julia Rothe was killed by the Grim Joker five weeks ago in her sittin'-room at Horsham. In the pocket of the Grim Joker's latest victim we find a five-pound note that at one time obviously belonged to the murdered woman. It seems to me to be interestin' and peculiar.'

'D'you think the Grim Joker put it there?' asked the young man. 'One of his distorted ideas of a joke?'

'Maybe.' The Rosebud folded the note and put it back in the wallet. 'I'd like to know, however, if he did, how he got hold of it in the first place.'

'Stole it when he killed the poor woman,' said Larry, but Mr. Budd shook his head.

'It wouldn't have been in her possession,' he replied. 'It's been changed somewhere — at a shop most probably, where they didn't know her. That's why she wrote her name and address on the back.'

'It's certainly strange,' mused Larry. 'However, we can talk about it later in more pleasant surroundings,' he added, shivering. 'At present all I want is to get out of this infernal wet.'

'We'll have to notify the local police about this.' Mr. Budd jerked his head towards the body. 'And get them to send an ambulance.' He turned to Leek. 'Go back to the house in the car and phone from there while I have a last look round, will you?' The sergeant nodded. 'And take those things with you,' added Mr. Budd.

He pointed to the small pile of personal belongings on the handkerchief.

While the sergeant wrapped up the contents of the pockets, Mr. Budd turned his attention to the body. Leek, looking more melancholy than ever, squelched his way through the mud to the gap in the hedge by which they had gained admittance to the field. He was saved going back to the house to ring up, however, for as he emerged into the roadway he saw a cyclist patrol coming steadily towards him. Waiting until he came abreast, Leek stopped the man and told him what had occurred.

'Murdered!' exclaimed the policeman incredulously. 'Dr. Roone!' He stared stupidly, mouth agape.

The thin sergeant nodded. 'Yes. Pretty bad business, too. Go back to your station and tell 'em to send an ambulance and the police surgeon. Tell the inspector-in-charge to come along, too.'

The dazed constable saluted, and remounting his machine went pedalling off swiftly in the direction whence he had come.

Going back to the others, Leek explained his lucky meeting with the policeman.

'Fine,' said Mr. Budd unenthusiastically. 'The sooner they send that ambulance, the better. There's nothin' more to be learned here, and I'm rather anxious to get back to the house.' He searched in his pocket and produced one of his cigars. Lighting it, he slowly exhaled a cloud of smoke and stared thoughtfully and sleepily at the skyline.

It seemed an eternity to Larry waiting in that sodden field before a jangling bell announced the arrival of the ambulance. With it came an inspector of police and a tall grave-faced man who proved to be the police surgeon for the district.

The brief preliminary introductions were soon got over, and after the superintendent had given a short account of what had occurred, Dr. Belbridge and the local inspector went over to the still form lying beneath the skeleton framework of the scarecrow. Bending down, the doctor gently lifted the handkerchief with which Mr. Budd had covered the head.

Drawing in his breath with a sharp hiss as he saw the injuries, he turned to the stout man.

'Good Lord!' he exclaimed in wonder and horror. 'This is dreadful! It looks as though some heavy instrument such as a hammer or similar object had been used.'

'Was that, in your opinion, the actual cause of death?' enquired Mr. Budd.

'Most certainly, I should say,' replied the doctor. 'Any one of these injuries would have proved fatal. The man who committed this crime must have been in a paroxysm of fury. It looks to me as if he continued to rain blow after blow long after life had ceased to exist.'

The stout superintendent nodded; but whether in agreement with the other's theory or some private idea of his own, it would have been difficult to judge.

The doctor finished his examination and began talking to Larry, while Mr. Budd was having a word with the local police officer.

'Poor Roone,' he said in a slightly hushed voice. 'I knew him quite well. Dreadful he should have died like this.'

'I knew him slightly,' said Larry. He gave a wry smile in which there was no mirth. 'I called this morning to ask him to come over to tea this afternoon.'

'He was a very nice fellow,' said Dr. Belbridge. 'A bit moody sometimes, but on the whole quite a good sort. Of course, I've read about this Grim Joker as they call him, and there's no doubt he's mad.'

'That's what everybody seems to think,' answered Larry. 'But he's sane enough to avoid capture. Poor Roone had a brother in Paris, hadn't he?'

'Yes,' replied Dr. Belbridge. 'I believe he had. He used to go and stay with him every now and again. Excuse me,' he added, turning as the local inspector called; and, leaving the young man, he went over to see what he wanted.

Larry strolled back to the police car while the body was being placed in the ambulance, and presently, when it had driven off with the inspector and the police doctor, Mr. Budd joined him. 'I'm glad that's over,' he grunted, huddling himself into the wet seat and wiping the back of his neck with his handkerchief. 'What I'd like more than anything else at the moment is a hot bath and a change of clothes.'

'I can give you the hot bath,' said Larry, 'but I'm afraid my clothes wouldn't fit.' He frowned. 'Breaking the news to Miss Grayson is going to be rather unpleasant.'

'I don't mind that so much,' said the stout man. 'It's when the news reaches the papers that's worryin' me. The fourth murder, and we're no nearer catchin' this jokin' feller than we ever were.'

'The only thing you seem near to catching is a cold,' answered Larry as the Rosebud ended with a prodigious sneeze.

A touch of blue had appeared in the sky, and the rain had almost ceased by the time they drew up in front of the covered porch and were greeted by the anxious face of Norma, who was standing in the doorway.

'Have you found anything?' she asked quickly; and then, as Larry nodded gravely, 'Not what you feared?'

'Worse, I'm afraid.'

She gave a little exclamation and her face went colourless.

'Let's go into the library,' Larry suggested, glancing at the figure of the butler who was lurking in a doorway near at hand.

Norma nodded, and in silence led the way up the staircase. In the big room she faced them, her back to the desk. 'Now tell me.' Her voice was the merest whisper, and without waste of time Mr. Budd gave her a brief outline of the tragedy.

'Horrible!' She shuddered and looked at the vacant chair before the open desk. 'Why, a few hours ago he was sitting there, and now — '

'I know,' said Larry gently as she turned away and sank into a chair by the fireplace.

'The fact that we were all more or less prepared for it makes it no less of a shock. Under the circumstances, I think you're wonderful.'

Mr. Budd, who had been looking dreamily at the window, turned slowly. 'I'm sorry to have to worry you,' he murmured, 'but there's one or two things I'd like to know.'

'I'll help you all I can,' she said.

'Well, for one thing,' said the stout man, 'I'd like the address of Dr. Roone's bankers.'

'I can give you that.' She rose to her feet and went over to the desk. 'Dr. Roone banked with the Southern Union, Piccadilly Branch,' she said, writing it down on a slip of paper.

'And who were his solicitors?'

'His solicitors were Sneed, Soames and Sneed of Bedford Row,' answered Norma, and added this to the address of the bank. She handed the paper to Mr. Budd.

'Thank you,' he said, folding it and putting it in his pocket. 'Now, what about this brother of his? Do you know his address?'

She shook her head. 'I'm afraid I don't, except that he lived somewhere in Paris. Dr. Roone used to receive letters from there and he told me they were from his brother.'

'I see.' The superintendent stifled a yawn. 'Probably we'll find some of these letters when we make a search of his belongings. Did you ever meet his brother?'

'Yes, he called here once,' she said with a nod, 'but he didn't stay very long. Dr. Roone told me that he'd come over to England on a visit and was leaving for Paris again the same night.'

'The doctor used to visit him now and again, didn't he?' asked Mr. Budd, and again she nodded.

'Yes, about once every six weeks,' she replied.

'And how long was he away on these visits?'

'Sometimes a week, sometimes a fortnight. More often only a week.'

Larry fidgeted impatiently. Why was the detective wasting time with these futile questions? he wondered. What did it matter how often Roone visited his brother?

If Mr. Budd noticed his impatience, he gave no sign. With half closed-eyes, he stood gently rubbing his chin. 'We'll have to find this fellow's address,' he said presently, 'and notify him of the tragedy.

Also, I'll have to get you to come down to the mortuary, Miss Grayson, and identify the body.'

'Oh,' she gasped. 'Is — is that really necessary?'

'I'm afraid it is. I'm sorry to have to ask you to do it. How long have you been with the doctor, Miss Grayson?' he added.

'A little over two years.'

'And what sort of a man was he to work for?'

'He was always most kind and considerate,' she answered, and there was a little catch in her voice.

'Yes, he struck me that way when I met him,' Mr. Budd said. 'He'd retired, hadn't he?'

'Yes. He didn't practise, if that's what you mean.'

'That's what I mean,' said the detective. 'So why did he require a secretary?'

'He was writing a book. A textbook on nervous diseases.'

'I see,' murmured the Rosebud thoughtfully; and then suddenly, to their surprise, he stepped quickly to the door, gripped the handle, and wrenched it open.

'You'll hear better inside,' he remarked as the sleek black-haired butler overbalanced and fell into the room.

9

The Man Who Escaped

The man scrambled to his feet, looking disconcerted. 'I was just coming to ask if you'd like any coffee,' he said, recovering himself.

'You were listenin' at the door,' accused Mr. Budd.

'You're mistaken, sir. I wouldn't do such a thing. I was stooping to straighten the mat.'

The stout man went over to the open door and peered down. There *was* a mat, and he grunted. 'Must have taken you a long time,' he remarked. 'You've been outside that door for the last three minutes.'

'No, sir,' Sellick said. 'I'm sorry to contradict you, but you've made a mistake. I had only just reached the door and was straightening the mat when you pulled it open.'

'Must have been mice I heard,' said the Rosebud sceptically.

'Yes, sir,' agreed Sellick smoothly, and turning to Norma: 'Would you like some coffee, miss?'

'Yes, I think I would,' she answered.

The butler bowed and withdrew, closing the door behind him.

'Was he listening?' asked Larry.

'I'm pretty sure of it,' answered Mr. Budd.

'I heard nothing,' said Norma.

'My hearin's exceptional,' murmured the Rosebud, 'an' I'm willin' to bet there was somebody outside that door for at least three minutes before I opened it.'

'Why should Sellick want to listen?' grunted Larry,

'I dunno,' the big man said. 'It's not unnatural he should be interested. Most people are interested in murder.'

Norma gave a little shiver. 'I can't realise it — even now,' she said. 'It doesn't seem real, somehow.'

'It's real right enough,' said Mr. Budd. 'There was nothin' illusionary about that poor feller when he was found. How long's this butler of yours been with you, Miss Grayson?'

'About two months.'

'Where did you get him? From one of the agencies?'

'No; he wrote to Dr. Roone and said that he had heard our butler was leaving on account of illness and asked for the situation. His references were excellent.'

'References mean nothin',' grunted the Rosebud. 'There are people in London who supply the finest references in the world for a fiver.'

'You don't think that Sellick has anything to do with . . . ' Norma began, alarmed.

'With this killin'?' interrupted Mr. Budd, and she nodded. 'I don't know who's had anythin' to do with it, but when I find a servant listenin' at a door I'm naturally suspicious.' He sighed wearily and yawned. 'Suppose we'd better have a look through Roone's papers,' he went on. 'I don't expect they'll help us much, but you never can tell.' He went to the door and called up Sergeant Leek, who had been left in the hall below, and together they began a search of the big desk.

Several of the drawers were locked, but Mr. Budd had brought with him the dead man's keys which he had taken from his clothing. Carefully and methodically, he and the long-faced sergeant examined every paper, but they found nothing helpful. There was, however, a bundle of letters from Roone's brother, and from these the fat man got his address in Paris.

In the middle of their investigations, Sellick came in with a tray of coffee, and they drank the steaming liquid gratefully.

While Mr. Budd and the sergeant were busy at the desk, Larry found an opportunity to talk to Norma. 'This will make a difference to you, won't it?' he said. 'I mean, you won't be staying on here.'

'I suppose I shan't,' she replied, and the worried expression on her face deepened.

There was dismay in her eyes, and he misconstrued the reason. 'I — I've been thinking of — of engaging a secretary for a long time,' he said untruthfully, for the thought had only that moment entered his head. 'I'd be awfully glad if you'd care to — ' He stopped, red and rather embarrassed.

'It's very kind of you, Mr. Weston,' she said gratefully, 'and I'd like to discuss it with you later. I shall certainly have to find another job when I leave here, which I suppose will be when Dr. Roone's brother takes charge.'

Inwardly congratulating himself on his brainwave, Larry nodded. 'His brother gets everything, I suppose?' he said.

'Yes,' she answered. 'Dr. Roone made a will a year ago. I know because I was one of the witnesses.'

'That's interestin'.' They were a little startled to hear Mr. Budd's lethargic voice close behind them. 'Who was the other witness, Miss Grayson?'

'Mr. Sneed,' said Norma.

'I'll be seein' *him* this afternoon,' Mr. Budd murmured sleepily.

Larry thought he looked very tired and despondent, but was sufficiently well acquainted with him to know that this meant nothing. Mr. Budd always appeared on the point of falling asleep, and never so much as when his brain was working at its fastest.

'There's nothin' more we can do here for the time bein',' said the superintendent presently, 'so I think I'll be gettin' along. I'll probably be back later, Miss Grayson, if it won't be troublin' you?'

'It won't trouble me at all,' she said.

'Then we'll go and wake up that driver of mine,' said the big man. 'Come along, Leek.' The melancholy sergeant accompanied his superior to the door.

'I must be getting back, too,' said Larry reluctantly, for he hated leaving Norma alone in that house of gloom. 'I've got an appointment with a man which I can't very well put off.'

Norma escorted them down the stairs to the hall. 'Thank you for everything,' she said, holding out her hand to Larry. 'You've been awfully kind.'

'I'm only too pleased to do anything I can,' he answered truthfully. 'And if there's any way I can help, you've only got to ring me up.'

She thanked him again. Mr. Budd had opened the front door, for there was no sign of the eavesdropping Sellick, when there came the sound of quick steps on the wet gravel of the drive. A thick-set, burly man was approaching rapidly, on his face a look of anxiety. Larry heard Norma give a gasp, and glancing at her sharply, he saw that her face had gone white and drawn.

The newcomer caught sight of them and increased his pace. 'Can I see Miss Grayson?' he demanded breathlessly; and then, as she moved into view: 'Oh, there you are. I'd like to speak to you privately.' His tone was urgent.

'Excuse me,' said Norma hurriedly, and taking the newcomer by the arm led him over to the staircase. 'Come up into the library.'

The burly man's voice floated back to them in a loud whisper as he ascended the stairs beside her. 'He got away when I wasn't looking . . . I thought perhaps he might have come here . . . '

His voice faded into an unintelligible mumble, but Mr. Budd and Larry had both heard that urgent whisper, and wondered. Who was the 'he' to whom the burly man referred? Apparently someone who had succeeded in escaping from somewhere. But why should the sight of this unprepossessing newcomer have thrown Norma into such a state of agitation? Neither the stout superintendent nor Larry made any remark, but they were both curious. Larry thought about nothing else as he drove slowly back to his own house, and Mr. Budd wondered throughout the journey to town.

10

Mr. Kyne Has a Visitor

Dusk was falling and a pale sliver of moon hung in the darkening sky when Sellick walked rapidly down New Bond Street, swung sharply into the side turning in which Mr. Kyne's sumptuous abode was situated, and entered the vestibule. The lift took him quickly to the fourth floor, and Mr. Kyne's polished front door was opened in answer to his knock by the acid-faced maid.

'Good evening,' said Sellick pleasantly. 'You grow more beautiful every time I see you.'

'You're too fresh!' she snapped, her black eyes blazing with anger.

'I've come straight off the ice!' he retorted, and chuckled as she flounced away. He was still chuckling when, after a short interval, she returned and held open the door.

'Come in,' she said ungraciously. 'Mr. Kyne will see you.'

'He undoubtedly will, unless he's gone blind,' said Sellick, entering. 'Thank you for your kindness in acting as an ambassador, or whatever is the female equivalent.'

She took no notice of his chaff, but led the way to the door of the study.

Mr. Kyne was reading the evening newspaper, and he folded this carefully and laid it aside as his visitor entered. 'Sit down, my dear Sellick,' he greeted, waving a hand towards a chair opposite him. 'Sit down. How did you manage to get away?'

'I told the Grayson woman that I had to meet a relative who was coming from the north,' answered Sellick, lighting a cigar which he took without permission from a box on the table. 'I suppose you saw an account of the affair in the papers?'

The smooth man nodded. 'Yes, the evening editions are humming with it,' he said. 'Directly I read of the murder, I guessed you'd be up. We seem to have had all our trouble for nothing.'

'I think we should have done that in any case,' said the late Dr. Roone's butler bitterly. 'There was nothing in the house worth taking away.'

'Hm.' Mr. Kyne frowned and pursed his lips. 'I was told that Roone was a rich man, a very rich man. I thought it was a cert to plant you there.'

'Whoever told you Roone was rich is a bigger liar than you are,' said Sellick coolly, 'and that's saying a lot. Roone was on the verge of bankruptcy. I reckon this Grim Joker man did him a good turn when he bumped him off.' He exhaled a cloud of blue smoke towards the gilded ceiling.

'Well, I suppose it can't be helped,' sighed Mr. Kyne resignedly. 'The best plans are apt to go awry. We made a mistake, that's all. I certainly thought we should be able to clear a nice little profit, with your skill as a draughtsman and access to his cheque-book. However, let's forget it.' He leaned forward and folded his hands on the blotting-pad. 'The Duchess of Dinely is looking for a new footman,' he went on quickly, 'and the Dinely Diamonds are beautiful.' He spread his hands expressively and winked. 'I've got all the references you'll want, and you can leave your present job at once. Give the murder as an excuse — '

'Not so fast,' interrupted Sellick. 'I'll leave my present job as soon as you like, but I'm doing no more lackey work yet awhile.'

'But, my dear fellow,' protested Mr. Kyne, 'this is a cinch — a certainty!'

'It may be, but I've got something better,' retorted the butler.

'Better than the Dinely Diamonds?' said Kyne in a hushed voice.

'Yes!' Sellick pulled his chair closer and leaned across the writing-table. 'Suppose I tell you that I know who the Grim Joker is?' he said impressively.

Mr. Oswald Kyne stared at him, his jaw dropped and his mouth an O of startled surprise. 'You know who the Grim Joker is?' he repeated slowly, after a long silence.

'I do,' Sellick replied, and dropping his voice to a whisper: 'I saw the murder committed, Kyne!'

'Good God!' The money-lender lay back limply in his chair, and his forehead glistened in the light.

'The police haven't the ghost of a clue yet,' Sellick continued. 'I was listening at the door of the library while they were talking to the Grayson woman, until that blasted 'busy' caught me.'

'Caught you?' Mr. Kyne's voice was anxious.

'Oh, you needn't worry,' said Sellick impatiently. 'I got out of it all right. I said I'd only just arrived and was straightening the mat; pretended I'd come to ask them if they wanted any coffee.' He laughed harshly. 'I think they believed me.'

Mr. Kyne took out an expensive silk handkerchief and wiped his suddenly damp face. 'This is a very extraordinary statement you've made. You're sure you're not mistaken?'

'I tell you I saw the murder committed, and I know who this fellow is the police are after.'

'We — we must have a serious talk.' The podgy hand of the man was shaking as he replaced the handkerchief in his breast pocket. 'A very serious talk.'

'That's what I'm here for. You can talk as seriously as you like, but what I'm after is money — big money.'

'Yes, yes, naturally,' muttered Mr. Kyne, passing his tongue over his lips, which had suddenly gone dry. 'Who — who do you think the Grim Joker is?'

'I don't think — I know!' snapped Sellick. 'And he's got to pay me a pretty big sum to keep my knowledge to myself.' He lowered his voice, and leaning forward whispered something.

Kyne's flaccid face flushed till the veins stood out in his temples with some suppressed emotion. For nearly two minutes he stared at Sellick in silence, a silence broken only by the ticking of the silver clock that stood beside the blotting pad. Then he rose unsteadily to his feet, and, going over to the door, locked it.

'How much is it worth?' he asked, coming back to the desk.

'Fifty thousand pounds?' suggested Sellick.

Mr. Kyne's lips pursed. 'Don't let's be

rash,' he said gently. 'We've got to talk this thing over.'

For close on an hour they remained whispering together, their heads almost touching. Eleven was striking when Sellick emerged from the entrance to the block of flats, and he was smiling as though well-satisfied with his evening's work.

Had he seen the figure that appeared from the shadow of the next doorway as he went off up the street, he would not have felt so pleased; for the trailer had been at his heels when he entered Mr. Oswald Kyne's ornate and luxurious abode, had waited patiently for him to come out, and was now following cautiously in his wake as he turned the corner.

11

The Millionaire Who Vanished

The great bell in the clock tower of the Houses of Parliament struck midnight, and the sound floating in through the open window of Mr. Budd's bare office at Scotland Yard caused that stout individual to stretch himself with a sigh of weariness.

He had been a very busy man since returning from Dorking that afternoon. He had visited Dr. Roone's bankers and also Messrs. Sneed, Soames and Sneed of Bedford Row, and the net result of his labours had given him a great deal to think about.

The dead man's affairs were in a decidedly chaotic state. There was very little balance at his bank; and according to Mr. Harold Sneed — an elderly, rusty man and the senior partner of his firm of lawyers — writs were out against him everywhere, and bankruptcy proceedings were imminent. Roone had been quite well off — a rich man in fact — less than two years previously, but an unfortunate speculation on the stock exchange which should have brought him a huge fortune went wrong and swallowed up nearly the whole of his capital.

He had left a will, which was in the possession of the solicitors, in which he appointed his brother sole executor and residuary legatee. But it didn't appear as if the brother — James Roone, who lived in a small flat in the Rue Douane, Paris — was likely to benefit at all. The dead man's debts amounted to over sixty thousand pounds, and his total assets were not a tenth of that sum.

Mr. Sneed had wired acquainting James Roone of his brother's tragic death, and had received in reply a telegram from his housekeeper. It appeared that her employer was away on a tour with some friends; but as soon as he returned, which she expected would be in about a week's time, he would communicate with the lawyers. She stated that she could not get in touch with him sooner because he was on a walking tour and she had no knowledge of his whereabouts.

So much had Mr. Budd gleaned from his enquiries, and interesting as it was, it brought him no nearer to solving the mystery of the Grim Joker, or helped him at all in discovering the identity of that weird and elusive personality.

There was one slight piece of evidence he had picked up in that field of death, and which he had kept to himself, that seemed to point to only one conclusion; and at the time he had been convinced that it was the right one. But his efforts to find some substantiating facts had so far met with failure. And not only that: the few facts he had found definitely clashed with his shadowy preconceived idea.

He reached in his pocket for one of his cigars and was in the act of lighting it when the door opened and a tall broad-shouldered, grey-haired man came in.

'Hello, Larne!' said Mr. Budd sleepily. 'Thought you'd gone home a long time ago.'

'Shan't get home yet awhile,' Larne grumbled. 'I've got to wade through a mass of reports on that Barllard business. Carling tells me you've got a list of all the disappearances during the last year. He sent it up to you yesterday, and you haven't returned it.'

'That's right,' said the Rosebud, and he searched among the mass of reports and folders that littered his desk. Selecting one, he pushed it across to Chief Inspector Larne. 'Any news of Barllard?' he asked.

Larne shook his head. 'No, there's not a sign of him. Heaven knows what could have happened to him!'

He referred to the mysterious disappearance of Austin Barllard, the tobacco millionaire. Six months previously he had left his house at Esher one morning with the intention of going for his usual walk which he invariably took at ten o'clock. He had never returned, and although the police were informed and search parties scoured the neighbourhood no trace had been found of him, then or since. On the morning of his disappearance he had been in the best of health and spirits.

Chief Inspector Larne had worked patiently and diligently without finding anything that offered an explanation for the millionaire's disappearance. He had lived a quiet life at the big house at Esher and was something of a recluse. So far as could be ascertained, he had no relatives. He had, in fact, been a foundling and started life as a newspaper boy, acquiring his millions by sheer industry and business acumen. There was nothing in his life to suggest a reason for his vanishing in such an extraordinary fashion. The police suspected foul play, but no body had been found; and from the time the missing man had started on his walk to the present, no trace of him had been discovered.

'You seem to be in the same boat as I am,' said Mr. Budd wearily as Larne picked up the folder and moved towards the door. 'You can't get a line on this vanishin' feller, an' I can't find anythin' to lead me to the Grim Joker.'

'Perhaps Barllard's the Grim Joker,' suggested Larne humorously. 'They both have this in common — that it's impossible to find either of them.'

He went out, leaving the Rosebud smoking thoughtfully. Presently Leek came in, looking more miserable than ever.

'That feller who's been trailin' Sellick's just reported,' said the sergeant. 'He picked him up at Roone's house early this evening and followed him up to town. Seems pretty certain the man's a crook. At nine o'clock he went to see Oswald Kyne. That feller only has two kinds of visitors, and Sellick ain't one of his victims.'

Mr. Budd was interested. He knew the smooth Mr. Kyne. He was one of the numerous people in London whom Scotland Yard regarded as suspicious. Nothing definite had ever been discovered against him, but he came into the category of an 'undesirable'.

'Went to see Kyne, did he?' murmured Mr. Budd. 'Hm! Put another man on to watch Kyne. You've still got somebody watching Sellick, I suppose?'

The sergeant nodded.

'Well, see that he isn't lost sight of. It may lead to nothin', but we can't afford to take any chances. That feller Sellick may be a crook, but I doubt if he's going to help us much.'

In this he was wrong, for fate had so arranged it that the humble Sellick was destined to lead him to the heart of the mystery, and in doing so save the lives of at least two innocent actors in the sinister drama, the final scene of which was at that moment being set.

12

The Man of the Night

Norma Grayson sat by the open window of her room, a novel on her knee, a reading lamp by her elbow. From the garden below came the pungent scent of flowers, accentuated by the rain of the morning.

She had been trying to read, but her troubled thoughts had obtruded themselves and she found it impossible. The horror of the tragedy still lay heavily upon her, and in addition she had a worry of her own that filled her with uneasiness.

She glanced out into the semi-darkness of the summer night and saw across the broad lawn the dark bulk of the shrubbery and the enclosing trees. Away beyond lay the cause of her uneasiness and fear.

There came a tap at the door, and a maid entered with a glass of hot milk.

'Has Sellick returned?' asked Norma as the woman set the glass down on the table beside her.

'Not yet, miss.'

Norma frowned and glanced at the little watch on her wrist. It was getting on for twelve, and the butler had promised to be back at eleven. 'All right,' she said, 'you needn't wait up.' The maid thanked her, wished her good night, and departed.

Putting her book aside, Norma sipped her milk and gave herself up to her thoughts. It was ten minutes past twelve when she heard the crunch of feet on the gravel below, and rising, she went downstairs just as Sellick let himself in.

'I'm sorry I'm late, miss, but I missed my train,' the butler apologised.

Norma thought she detected a trace of excitement in his face. His eyes were brighter than usual, and there was a flush to his sallow skin. She wondered if he had been drinking.

She gave him a few instructions for the morning and turned to re-ascend the stairs. Halfway up she turned, for no reason at all, and looked back. Sellick was

114

still standing in the middle of the hall watching her, and there was such a peculiar expression on his face that for an instant she felt frightened.

She almost ran the rest of the way, and reached her room a little breathless. The remainder of her milk was cold but she drank it, and locking her door went over to the window and stood, looking out into the darkness. She was trying to find a reason for the peculiar sneering smile she had surprised on the butler's face. Did he know?

Her reason told her that he couldn't; and yet, if he was capable of listening at the door, he was capable of other deceptions. Perhaps on those occasions when she had slipped out at night he had followed her. She gave a little jerk to her shoulders. Well, it didn't matter very much now.

As she undressed slowly, she heard him locking up downstairs, and presently his soft footsteps passed her door as he went up to his own room.

She had never felt less like sleep in her life, and for a long time she drifted aimlessly about the room in her dressing gown. The house seemed very still and lonely. She could hear the faint sound of the wind in the trees, but otherwise it was very quiet. It was after one when she reluctantly slipped out of her dressing gown and got into bed. Switching out the light, she lay for a long time, her thoughts revolving over and over again round the same thing. Eventually she must have fallen asleep, for she knew no more until she suddenly found herself sitting up in bed listening intently.

Something must have occurred to have roused her from her sleep. She strained her ears, but there was no sound in the silent house, nor was there any sound outside. The wind had dropped.

Suddenly she became aware that the silence of the house had been broken. There stole up to her from somewhere below a faint sound — the squeak of a hinge. Norma knew that sound well. It came from the library door!

With all her senses alert, she got stealthily out of bed, and drawing on her dressing gown over her nightdress slid her feet into a pair of slippers. Cautiously she went to the door and opened it. The corridor outside was in darkness and she had to feel her way to the stairs. Leaning over the bannister, she peered down at the landing below. There was no sound now, but she thought she caught sight of a faint flicker of light that gleamed for a moment from the direction of the library.

Very softly and carefully, she began to make her way down the staircase and succeeded in reaching the lower landing without making a sound. The library door, which she had closed before coming up to bed, was now wide open, and from her position she could see into the room. A man was bending over the big desk. He had his back towards her and appeared to be searching for something by the light of an electric lamp that he carried.

Norma thought quickly. It would be useless for her to tackle the intruder. She could not hope to pit her strength against his. The first thing that occurred to her was to arouse the butler, but her newly born distrust of the man prevented her from carrying this out.

What could she do? Suddenly Larry's words came back to her, and she thought of the telephone. There was an extension instrument in Dr. Roone's bedroom, which was at the end of the corridor in which her own room was situated.

Cautiously she began to make her way back up the stairs. There was one halfway up the flight which creaked. She knew this, and coming down she had avoided it, but now in her excitement she trod on the stair before she realised what she had done. It gave a protesting crack, with a noise that sounded to her ears like a pistol shot.

She stopped dead, wondering if the man below had heard it. Apparently he had not, for listening, the gentle rustling of papers came to her ears.

She continued on her way, and reaching the door of the doctor's room she opened it and stepped across the threshold. She was afraid to risk a light and felt her way round the bed towards the little table on which stood the telephone. Feeling for the instrument, she lifted the receiver.

Larry had given her his number, which luckily she remembered. In as low a voice as possible, she gave it to the exchange operator and waited. Her wisest course would have been to call the local police station, but this never even occurred to her.

It seemed to her strained nerves an age before she heard Larry's voice come sleepily over the wire. 'Is that Mr. Weston?' she asked in a low tone. 'This is Norma Grayson. Mr. Weston, there is somebody — ' There was a crackling noise in the receiver. 'Hello!' she called. 'Can you hear me?' But there was no reply.

Concluding that she had been cut off at the exchange, she rattled the hook urgently, but there was no accompanying click in the earpiece. And then, while she was still trying to get an answer from the exchange, the door behind her opened. She heard a rush of feet, and the instrument was snatched from her hand.

'If you scream,' said a high-pitched voice, 'I'll kill you, the same as I killed Roone!'

She almost fainted, for the high-pitched voice was the same as the voice that had come over the wire that morning!

A pair of strong hands gripped her by the throat, and she felt herself forced back onto the bed. Desperately she beat with her fist in the face of her attacker; but the grip on her throat, instead of relaxing, grew tighter. She felt the blood pounding in her head, and her senses swam — and then suddenly consciousness left her, and she knew nothing.

13

The Secret Drawer

Larry Weston, still dazed with sleep, heard the sudden break in Norma's voice, and called frantically into the mouthpiece of his telephone. 'Hello! Hello!' But there was no reply.

With a muttered curse, he reached over and pressed the switch, and after a long interval heard the voice of the exchange operator asking him what number he wanted.

'I don't want any number,' said Larry. 'Someone was speaking to me when you cut us off.'

'Hang up your receiver,' said the operator unemotionally, when he had ascertained that Larry had not made the call. 'They'll ring you again.'

Larry banged the instrument back in its rack. He was wide awake now, and a little alarmed. For what reason had Norma rung him up in the middle of the night? A glance, at his watch showed him that it was nearly three.

He swung himself out of bed and pulled on his dressing gown, listening intently for the telephone to ring again, but it remained silent.

At last he could curb his impatience no longer, and going down to his small study he found the telephone directory and hastily looked up Dr. Roone's number. Coming back to his bedroom, he called the exchange, only to be informed that the number was unobtainable.

'What do you mean, unobtainable?' he snapped angrily. 'They rang me up a few minutes ago.'

'I'm sorry,' said the weary voice of the operator, 'but something seems to have gone wrong with the line.'

Larry's face whitened. He was now thoroughly alarmed. It looked as though something serious had occurred at the Larches. Unless the matter had been very urgent, Norma would never have rung him up in the first place at that hour.

He wasted no more time, and began

hastily to dress himself. Ten minutes later, rather sketchily attired, he was getting his little car out of the garage.

It was ten minutes past three when he came up the drive of Dr. Roone's house and brought his car to a halt at the main entrance. Everything was very still and quiet. There was no sign of life to be seen. No light gleamed from any of the windows, and the hall was in darkness.

Hurrying up the steps, he searched for the bell, and pressed the button. He heard it ringing faintly somewhere inside the house and waited, but there was no reply to his summons. He rang again and added a thunderous tattoo on the knocker.

At length a light sprang up in the hall and he heard the shuffling of footsteps. The rattle of a chain and the rasp of bolts being drawn back reached him, and then the door was opened and the butler, clad in a dingy dressing gown, blinked at him.

'What's the matter?' he began ungraciously. 'Who the — ' And then he recognised Larry and his jaw dropped in surprise.

'What's been happening here?' snapped Larry quickly.

'Happening, sir?' said the sleepy-eyed butler. 'I don't know what you mean.'

Larry pushed past him into the hall. 'Miss Grayson tried to ring me up half an hour ago,' he said curtly, 'and something happened to prevent her.'

Briefly he explained. The butler's face grew more astonished. 'I've only just woken up, sir,' he said. 'I've heard nothing.'

'Where's the telephone?' demanded Larry impatiently.

'There's one in the library, and there's an extension in the doctor's bedroom. I don't — '

But Larry wasn't listening. He was already ascending the stairs two at a time.

The library door was open and the room was in darkness. Pressing the switch, which was just inside the door, he gave a hurried glance round. There was nobody there.

'Show me the way to the doctor's bedroom,' he said as Sellick joined him, and the butler led the way up the stairs and along a corridor on the second floor. At the end of this he paused outside a closed door.

'Here you are, sir,' he said, and twisting the handle Larry opened the door and peered in.

As in the case of the library, the room was in darkness, but feeling along the wall he found the switch and pressed it down. As the room became flooded with light, an exclamation left his lips. Lying on the disordered bed was the motionless figure of Norma Grayson!

For one dreadful moment, Larry thought she was dead. But then he saw her irregular breathing, and going closer, the bruises on her throat . . .

'Get some water and some brandy,' he said to the surprised butler, 'and wake one of the female servants!'

The astonished Sellick hurried away, and Larry set to work to try and bring Norma back to consciousness. She had obviously been half-strangled, but when he had bathed her face and forced a few drops of the brandy, which the butler brought, between her lips, she opened her eyes. It was some time, however, before she had sufficiently recovered to be able to speak, and then she could only do so with difficulty and in a husky whisper. Larry listened to her story gravely.

'He must have heard you telephoning and cut the wire,' he said. 'I think the police ought to be informed at once.'

Norma agreed. Her throat ached horribly, and she was still a little dazed and frightened from her experience.

Larry handed her over to the care of the gaping housemaid, whom Sellick had hastily aroused, and went down to the library. The extension wires to the telephone upstairs ran from the bell, which was screwed to the wall, along the skirting board; and near the door they had been neatly severed. The main instrument on the desk, however, was in working order, and after some little difficulty Larry succeeded in getting through to Scotland Yard.

Mr. Budd had gone home, but after hearing Larry's story the officer in charge put him through to the inspector on night duty, and that individual promised to notify the superintendent immediately.

Going upstairs to report to Norma, Larry discovered her in her own room sipping a cup of hot coffee which the butler had prepared. Larry accepted a cup himself gratefully. 'You're sure this fellow was the same one who rang up Budd yesterday morning?' he asked.

She nodded. 'I'm certain. I couldn't mistake that voice.'

'What was he like?' asked Larry, but she could give no description of her assailant.

'I only saw his back in the library,' she replied, 'and it was quite dark in the bedroom when he attacked me.' She fingered her throat and shivered. 'He was very strong,' she went on. 'His fingers were like steel.'

'I wonder what he came for,' muttered the young man, frowning; but she could offer no suggestion.

'He seemed to be searching for something in the desk,' she said, 'but what it was I can't imagine.'

It was daylight when Mr. Budd arrived, a weary and sleepy-eyed man, for it had been in the early hours of that morning when he had reached his bed. He listened in silence while they told him what had happened.

'I remember most of the things in that desk,' he said. 'P'raps I'll be able to see whether he's taken anythin'.'

Larry accompanied him in his search, and it didn't take them long to discover the reason for the night intruder's presence. Two of the smaller drawers below the nest of pigeonholes in the roll-top desk had been pulled out. The space behind concealed a third and narrower drawer which had been left open.

'Empty,' said Mr. Budd laconically. 'Whatever it contained, that feller's taken it away with him.' He gazed thoughtfully at the secret drawer for some moments in silence, and then he sighed. 'Now let's see how he got in,' he murmured, and led the way downstairs.

An examination of the lower part of the house showed that the burglar had effected an entrance by one of the dining-room windows. It was of the casement pattern, with triangular leaded panes. One of these near the hasp had been pushed out.

'These windows are the burglar's delight,' remarked Mr. Budd sadly. 'He had only to put in his hand and raise the catch and the thing was done. You might just as well leave all the doors wide open and put up a welcome notice.'

'I wonder what was in that drawer,' said Larry.

'I'm wonderin' that, too,' remarked the Rosebud, 'but I'm wonderin' somethin' else a great deal more.'

'What's that?' asked Larry, but his question remained unanswered.

The intruder had left nothing behind him in the nature of a clue, and at half-past seven Mr. Budd took his leave of Larry and Norma and drove sadly and thoughtfully back to town in his disreputable little car. At a tea-shop near Westminster Bridge, he pulled up and ate a leisurely breakfast.

He had been hunched up in his chair behind his big office desk for nearly three hours, apparently finishing his interrupted sleep, when Chief Inspector Larne came to him. 'I think I've found something that'll interest you, Budd,' he said. 'I've just discovered it.' He laid a newspaper cutting, yellow with age, in front of the stout man, and Mr. Budd heaved himself laboriously into a sitting position. 'Read it,' said Larne.

The superintendent did so, and suddenly his sleepy eyes opened very wide indeed. The cutting was an account of a fire at the Metro-Palace Hotel, Brighton, which, according to the date, had happened fifteen years previously. After giving an account of the conflagration, the cutting ended:

'Among the few people saved from the burning building was Mr. Austin Barllard, the well-known tobacco millionaire. He was occupying a suite on the third floor; and, being a martyr to insomnia, he had taken a sleeping-draught before retiring. The drug was evidently a strong one, for the fire failed to wake him; and but for the heroic efforts of two fellow guests, Mr. Hamilton Lorne and Mr. Percival Haynes, he would have undoubtedly perished in the flames. As it was, he suffered a severe shock and several bad burns, and had to be rushed to the nearest hospital.'

'What do you think of that?' asked Larne.

'I think you've supplied me with the best clue I've had yet,' said Mr. Budd. 'It seems that at last we've established a connection between the first two victims of the Grim Joker.'

The Chief Inspector nodded. 'I thought you'd be interested,' he said. 'It looks very much to me as though there was a connection between these two cases, the disappearance of this fellow Barllard and this 'joking Johnnie'.'

Mr. Budd's eyes were very thoughtful as he nodded. 'He disappeared just two weeks before the Grim Joker killed Hamilton Lorne,' he murmured. 'Maybe there *is* a connection.'

He stared at the yellow cutting, his heavy lids drooping once more over his eyes. From it seemed to rise a faint mist which took the form of a terrifying figure; terrifying because it was faceless and had neither shape nor substance.

And somewhere in the back of his mind hovered four shapes even less tangible: a stockbroker, an architect, a doctor and an elderly spinster, who had been sacrificed to the perverted humour of the Grim Joker.

14

The Prisoner

The soft lapping sound of water washing against the wooden side of the boat woke the man who lay on a narrow pallet bed in the tiny cabin. He stirred uneasily, opening his eyes and staring into the pitch-blackness that surrounded him. The noise of the water was familiar, for it had been his constant companion for longer than he cared to think.

Turning with difficulty because of the manacles that confined his wrists and ankles, he lay on his back, moving his jaws as best he could to try and ease the ache and stiffness caused by the gag that was securely tied about his mouth.

Although the darkness was intense — by which he knew that night had fallen — he could picture every article of furniture in that small room. He knew every crack in the walls and ceiling and every mark on the threadbare, stained carpet, even down to the number of threads in its ravelled edge — for that had been his sole means of amusement during the hundred and five days he had been kept a prisoner in this place.

A hundred and five days! It seemed like as many years since he, Austin Barllard, had set out from his luxurious home for that morning walk and had been accosted by the bearded man with the limousine car who had enquired the way to town. The car had overtaken him on that deserted strip of country road, and he had approached the driver to give him the required directions when something had sprayed in his face. He remembered no more until he had recovered consciousness to find himself in his present surroundings.

The lapping water and the gentle swaying motion told him that he was on board some kind of boat. That it was moored somewhere was equally evident, since there was never any propulsive motion. But whose boat and where it was, he hadn't the remotest idea. That was the most extraordinary thing about the whole business.

The reason why he had been kidnapped, and the identity of his abductor, was a profound mystery; and rack his tired brain as he might, he could find no solution. At first he had concluded that the usual ransom was at the bottom of it, but the masked man who had brought him food and stood over him with a loaded pistol while he ate said nothing to confirm this idea. In fact he had never spoken at all, remaining deaf to his prisoner's questions and threats, until Austin Barllard had given up trying to extract any information from him.

For a long time he lay looking up into the darkness; and then, just as his weary eyes were closing and he was almost dropping off into a doze again, he heard the sound of a step outside. The boat rocked as someone came on board, and he heard the noise of heavy breathing. Presently there came the grating of a key in the lock, and a current of fresh, cool air blew on his face. Someone stumbled into the tiny cabin, and after a pause there was the scratch of a match.

As the yellow flame flickered to life, Barllard made out the dim form of his captor. The newcomer came over to the table which stood in the centre of the floor, and shielding the match from the draught of the open door, bent down and lit an oil lamp. It gave very little more light than the match, for the chimney was dirty; but it was sufficient for the millionaire to make out the packet the unknown had laid on the table.

Having lighted the lamp, the man, whose face was concealed by a coloured silk handkerchief knotted behind his head, locked the door; and, producing an automatic pistol and a bunch of keys from his pocket, he approached the man on the narrow mattress. Holding the pistol in his right hand, he stooped, unlocked the handcuffs round Barllard's wrists, and motioned to him to untie the gag.

This was the usual procedure to which use had now accustomed the millionaire. In complete silence the unknown backed to the table, keeping Barllard covered all the while with the pistol, and picking up the packet of sandwiches, turned and laid them by his side.

He watched while his prisoner struggled to a sitting posture and ate greedily, for this was his one meal of the day; and when he had finished, he replaced the handcuffs and snapped them shut. Going over to a cupboard in the corner, he fetched a thermos flask and poured into the cup-like cap some hot coffee. Coming back to the side of the helpless man, he held the cup while he drank, and then refilled it.

'How much longer are you going to keep me here?' asked the millionaire as the man in the mask returned the thermos flask to the cupboard.

The other remained dumb. He might as well have been speaking to himself for all the notice his remark elicited. Every night since he had been in this place, he had tried to engage the other in conversation, to learn, if possible, the reason for his confinement; but no word had the man ever spoken.

He shut the cupboard door, and

picking up the gag, carefully strapped it in place, testing it to see that it was secure. The automatic he had laid on the table he picked up and returned to his pocket; and then, going over to the door, he went out. Usually this meant that he was departing; but tonight, for some reason or other, he lingered. Barllard heard him moving about outside.

Presently, to the millionaire's surprise, he returned to the little cabin, took out a pen and ink from a drawer in the table, produced writing paper and envelopes, and pulling up a chair, sat down and began to write. He wrote slowly and carefully, pausing for long intervals to think. When he had finished, he read through what he had written, blotted it carefully, addressed an envelope, and, enclosing the sheet of paper, licked it down. Returning the pen, ink and paper to the drawer from which he had taken them, he closed it and stood for a moment, apparently deep in thought.

The millionaire watched him curiously. He would have given a lot to know the identity of this man, and a considerable sum to learn the reason for his own abduction. He had no idea that the figure before him was the Grim Joker who had spread such panic throughout the country, and whom every policeman was looking for; for the first public appearance of that individual had not taken place until after his incarceration in his present prison.

He was still puzzling his brains, as he had puzzled them many times before, to account for the motive behind the man's actions, when his gaoler straightened up and, turning, regarded him steadily over the top of the handkerchief bound about his face. And then suddenly, for the first time, he spoke — a high-pitched squeak that shook slightly as though with suppressed laughter. It was the voice more than the words he uttered that sent a little icy shiver down Barllard's spine.

'You're wondering why you're here,' said the Grim Joker, and he chuckled shrilly. 'Well, I'll tell you, he-he-he, but not yet. I'll tell you when the time is ripe. You asked me how long you're going to be here. Two more nights and two more days, he-he-he. Make the most of your time, for it is very short. At twelve o'clock the night after tomorrow, you die!' He chuckled again and blew out the lamp.

15

The Wild Man

Larry Weston had promised Norma before he had left in the morning that he would come back that evening. He had said that he would stroll over at about nine o'clock, but it was half past eight when he left his house and took the short cut across the intervening fields that separated his own domain from the Larches, and a quarter to nine when he reached his destination.

In answer to his ring, Sellick opened the door. 'Miss Grayson isn't in,' said the man in reply to his enquiry. 'She went out immediately after dinner.'

Larry was a little disconcerted. Had the woman forgotten he was calling? Certainly he was early. He had mentioned nine, and it wanted a quarter of an hour to that time.

'I don't know how long she'll be, sir,'

said the butler, seeing his hesitation. 'Perhaps you'd like to wait?'

He ushered the young man into the big drawing-room and left him. Larry strolled over to the window and looked out across Dr. Roone's neatly laid-out garden. He was a little piqued that Norma had not been at home to receive him. He knew that this was unreasonable. He made no secret to himself of the attraction she had for him. Since that accidental meeting in the post office, she had rarely been out of his thoughts. In spite of the fact that they had only met three or four times, she had become a necessary adjunct to his life. He told himself severely that he was behaving like a callow schoolboy. So far as he knew, Norma Grayson might be already engaged; and, anyway, there was no reason why she should feel in the least degree interested in him.

He was still standing gazing out of the window, his mind occupied with not-unpleasant speculations concerning the future, when Norma came in. She had been hurrying and was a little breathless, but Larry was too concerned about her appearance to notice signs that should have been very flattering to his vanity. Her face was pale and drawn, and there were worried lines about her eyes and in her smooth forehead. She was full of apologies for being out when he had arrived, but Larry waved them aside.

'It was my fault,' he said. 'I was early.'

She took off her hat and coat and rather wearily tidied her hair. 'It was very good of you to come at all,' she said. She sank down in a chair by the flower-filled fireplace, and Larry perched himself on the corner of the settee.

'I hadn't been out all day,' she went on, 'and I began to feel a little stuffy and headachy, so I thought I'd go for a stroll.'

She made the explanation haltingly, and for some reason or other Larry was convinced that she was lying. The reason she had given was not the true one. He dismissed the thought almost as soon as it entered his head, and searching his mind for something to say, remembered an item of news that Mrs. Clipp had imparted that morning.

'We had a burglary, too, last night,' he said.

She looked at him quickly. 'A burglary?' she repeated. 'Surely it couldn't have been the same man?'

He shook his head and chuckled. 'I don't think so. My burglar forced the pantry window and stole three bottles of whisky — ' He broke off in concern as he caught sight of Norma's face. She was staring at him, horror-stricken.

'Say that again,' she whispered huskily.

'Why, what's the matter? I'm terribly sorry if I've said anything to frighten you.'

She recovered herself with an effort. 'It's nothing,' she said, and reached towards the box beside her for a cigarette, but her hand was shaking and her whole appearance belied her words. 'It was silly of me. You say he took three bottles of whisky?'

'Yes. I don't suppose it was a burglar at all; more likely some tramp on the lookout for anything he could pick up. The whole thing was very clumsily done. The glass of the window was smashed. It's a wonder my housekeeper and her husband didn't hear anything.'

Norma's momentary panic had subsided. Her face was still pale, and at the back of her eyes was a trace of fear, but her voice had recovered its steadiness. 'I expect it was a tramp,' she agreed. 'It couldn't have been the man who broke in here.'

'No, I'm certain it wasn't,' Larry said reassuringly. 'The Grim Joker certainly wouldn't take the trouble to steal three bottles of my whisky.' Rather tactfully he changed the subject, leading the conversation into other channels.

It was dusk when he took his leave; a still, warm night, with a star-sprinkled sky that was rapidly turning to ultramarine. Larry whistled softly to himself as he strolled back along the winding lane that would eventually bring him to his own home.

During the latter part of their conversation, he had re-opened the subject of the offer of becoming his secretary, and Norma had more than gratefully accepted. It had been arranged that she should come to him at the end of the month, and he was absurdly pleased at the thought of having her fragrant personality constantly beside him. Once she had left the Larches, the tragedy with which she had been associated would be forgotten. He hated to see that worried, drawn look about her eyes.

He came to the end of the lane and plunged into the depths of the little wood that lay between it and the boundary of his grounds. It was very dark here, for the trees grew thickly, and their leafy branches formed an impenetrable roof through which no ray of starlight could percolate. The darkness did not trouble Larry, however, for he knew every inch of the way. Since he had taken the house, he had spent a lot of time in this little wood, and in his imagination had planned many a garden in its cool quietness. On a summer morning it was a place of translucent greens and yellow sunlight, filled with the song of birds and gay with woodland flowers. Here in the spring were to be found wild violets and primroses, bluebells and anemones clustering at the feet of the tree trunks.

Larry had reached the centre of the

footpath which zig-zagged its way through the wood when he heard a sound like someone moving among the undergrowth in front. Although he seldom used it, he invariably carried an electric torch in his pocket when he went out at night, and feeling for this now he withdrew it and pressed the button. In the fan-shaped light that cut the darkness, he saw a figure cross the path in front of him, and focused it in the ray.

'Don't do that!' screamed a hoarse voice. 'Put that light out. Damn you, put that light out!'

The speaker was a gaunt man clad in a pair of shapeless flannel trousers and a soiled tennis shirt. His face was covered with a stubbly growth of beard; and his eyes, red and blinking, glared at Larry venomously from sunken sockets.

'Who are you?' he demanded curtly. 'You've no right here!'

The wild man bared his teeth in a snarl. 'You leave me alone,' he screamed; and his hand, flying to his hip pocket, reappeared with an ugly-looking knife. 'You're one of the enemy. I know you!

This wood's full of them, but you won't get me again!' He broke into a torrent of bad language and crouched, the knife held defensively before him.

Larry was both astonished and alarmed. The man was obviously mad, but who he was and where he had come from he hadn't the least idea. 'Look here — ' he began, making a step forward; but at the movement the other gave a hoarse scream and sprang at him. Larry knocked aside the wild thrust of his knife, and with a string of curses the man turned and fled into the depths of the wood.

For a second Larry stood undecided. His first impulse was to follow and try and catch the man, for it might be dangerous to leave this armed lunatic at large in the neighbourhood. In fact, he had taken three or four steps in the other's direction before he realised the futility of any attempt to find him. The wood was dense, and bushes grew thickly everywhere, except where the little path bisected it. If the man was cunning, it would be next to impossible to find him, and in searching he stood a very good risk of getting that unpleasant-looking knife in his back. He determined, however, immediately he got home, to ring up the police station and inform them of his adventure. He kept a sharp lookout as he covered the rest of the way, but there was no other sight or sound of the wild man, and he reached the security of his house without further shocks or surprises.

The sergeant at Dorking Police Station listened to what he had to say, asked one or two questions, and promised that the matter should be looked into. There had been no notice of any lunatic having escaped, and the sergeant, like Larry, was at a loss to account for the presence of the man in the neighbourhood.

It was not until he had hung up the receiver and turned away from the instrument that it occurred to Larry that here was an explanation of the burglary of the previous night, and the theft of his three bottles of whisky. He called Mrs. Clipp and her husband and questioned them, but neither of them knew of anyone in the neighbourhood who remotely resembled Larry's description of the gaunt man in the shirt and trousers.

'Maybe 'e's the chap everyone's lookin' for, sir,' suggested Mr. Clipp, 'this 'ere Grim Joker feller wot did in the doctor.'

Larry started. This hadn't crossed his mind. The man certainly appeared mad, and he was in the neighbourhood.

When his two servants had gone, he sat down to consider Mr. Clipp's suggestion. It was feasible but rather improbable. The Grim Joker's crimes had been carried out with a cunning which at first glance seemed beyond the capacity of the wild-looking man he had met in the wood. And yet madmen were notoriously cunning.

When eventually tiredness forced him to seek his bed, he had made up his mind. On the morrow he would acquaint Mr. Budd with the incident in the wood and shift whatever responsibility there might be from his shoulders to the broader ones of the stout superintendent.

16

Mr. Budd Receives the Warning

Larry reached Scotland Yard at eleven o'clock on the following morning, and leaving his little car in the quadrangle before the entrance, passed into the grim building. With a nod to the sergeant on the door, who knew him well, he ascended the stone stairs until he came to Mr. Budd's office.

That stout individual was apparently taking a nap when he entered, for he was lounging back in the chair behind his desk, his eyes closed, and his hands folded comfortably over his capacious stomach. He opened one eye as Larry entered and gave a grunt of surprise.

'Hello!' he said. 'What are you doin' here?'

'I've got some news for you,' said Larry, closing the door and pulling forward a chair.

'Everybody seems to have got news for me,' grunted Mr. Budd, 'but most of it's ancient history.' He sighed. 'Let's hear what you've got to say.'

Larry told him briefly, and there was no doubt as to the superintendent's interest. 'It's certainly worth lookin' into,' he remarked, yawning, when the young man had finished his story, 'but I don't think this feller you met in the wood is the Grim Joker.'

'I came to that conclusion myself, but I thought it was just as well to tell you about him.'

'All contributions of information are thankfully received,' murmured the stout man. 'An' now, I'll give you some.' Slowly and ponderously, as was his wont, he acquainted his friend with Chief Inspector Larne's discovery. 'I've been enquirin' into this Brighton fire business,' he said, 'and I've found out somethin' that's both interestin' an' peculiar.'

'What's that?' asked the interested Larry.

'I've found out the names of the doctor and the nurse who attended this man

Barllard after he'd been rescued by Larne and Haynes and taken to hospital.'

'It doesn't seem to me to be important, but I suppose it is.'

'You suppose rightly,' said the stout man, 'because the doctor's name was Roone and the nurse's name was Julia Rothe!'

'Good Lord!' The astonishment on Larry's face was ludicrous. 'That establishes a connection between all four victims of the Grim Joker.'

'It does,' agreed Mr. Budd, nodding. 'An' it establishes somethin' else. It establishes the fact that this fire which destroyed the Metro-Palace Hotel at Brighton gave birth to the Grim Joker.'

Larry frowned, a little puzzled. 'I don't get what you mean.'

'I mean,' replied the Rosebud, 'that somethin' which occurred either durin' or after that fire was the startin' point — the motive behind all these apparently meaningless murders.'

'But you said the fire happened fifteen years ago!'

Mr. Budd nodded again rather wearily.

'I know I did, but all the same it's at the bottom of the whole business. I'm not sayin' I know how or why, but it's the one obvious point of contact that connects all the people this feller's killed.'

Larry scratched his chin. 'It may do that, but it still seems utterly mad.'

'Maybe it does, but it isn't,' said the superintendent. 'And neither is this Jokin' feller mad. I had a hunch he wasn't all along. I should say he was the nearest approach to the perfect criminal that we're ever likely to come up against.'

Larry pursed his lips. 'I'm still of the opinion that he's a homicidal lunatic.'

'You're with the majority, but I'll tell you somethin'. Has it ever struck you that that's the impression he's tryin' to create?'

Larry started, and the stout man smiled slowly. 'These theatrical warnin's with the figure of the laughin' fool; these unnecessary rhymes, obviously ridiculous and pointin' conclusively to a distorted brain. And, when he rang me up, this disguised voice interspersed with those little cacklin' chuckles — all carefully prepared to give me the impression that I was dealin' with a maniac.' He shook his head sadly. 'No, Larry, the Grim Joker is a clever man with a real purpose hidin' behind this sinister nonsense of his. He's tried to throw dust in the eyes of the police and the public, but so far as I'm concerned he hasn't succeeded.'

'When you put it like that, I begin to believe you're right,' said Larry thoughtfully.

'I know I'm right,' murmured the stout man immodestly. 'I've been right all the time. The only thing I haven't got as yet is the motive behind all this business. Once I've got that, the case is over.'

'You mean that the motive will also give you the identity of the Grim Joker?'

'I don't mean any thin' of the sort. I *know* the identity of the Grim Joker.'

'What!' gasped Larry in astonishment.

'I pretty well know who this Jokin' feller is,' went on Mr. Budd, 'but until I find out what's behind it all, and why these people were killed, I couldn't prove it.'

'Who *is* he?' demanded the young man,

recovering from his surprise.

'I don't think I'm goin' to tell you that. Not at present, at any rate. I might be wrong, and then I'd look foolish. Not that I think I am,' he added.

Larry grunted.

'I can see you're a bit sceptical,' Mr. Budd went on. 'But I'm going to continue to risk your disbelief until I've got somethin' more like proof.'

There was a tap at the door and a messenger came in. He laid half a dozen letters on the desk in front of Mr. Budd and withdrew. The stout man, with a muttered apology, picked them up and glanced through them. His eyes narrowed as he came to a large square envelope addressed in a sprawling childish hand. Ripping open the flap, he withdrew a card bearing on it the drawing of the familiar fool with the pointing index finger!

'I thought it wouldn't be long before I got one of these,' he murmured.

Larry, who had been pondering over his previous remark, looked up. 'What is it?' he asked; and then, as he saw what the stout man held between his fingers: 'The Grim Joker!'

Mr. Budd nodded slowly. There was a queer look on his face as he turned the card over and read the doggerel verse on the back.

Though sleepy and lazy and fat,
You're possessed of a brain for all
   that.
You're a danger, and so
I am letting you know
Curiosity once killed a cat.

Mr. Budd tossed the card over to Larry and sighed wearily. 'He's gettin' scared,' he remarked.

Larry read the limerick and looked up. 'What are you going to do?'

Mr. Budd's eyes twinkled slightly. 'I'm goin' to apply for police protection!' he answered.

17

The Appointment

The sleek-haired Mr. Sellick, waiting at Dorking station for the train that was to carry him townwards, felt remarkably good-tempered and at peace with the world. The reason for his amiability was due to the telephone message he had received that morning from his friend Mr. Oswald Kyne.

Mr. Kyne had given him a piece of news that filled the soul of the butler with rapturous dreams of wealth. Over and over again he congratulated himself upon the foresight that had made him follow Dr. Roone when he had left the house that fatal morning in response to the Grim Joker's faked telephone call. But for that piece of luck, he would never have witnessed the crime, and thus held its perpetrator in the hollow of his hand; for — and Mr. Sellick chuckled as he always did when he thought of this — the murder had already been committed when Superintendent Budd had arrived at the house, and it was only by a matter of seconds that he had himself returned in time to admit him.

He was still chuckling when he got into a third-class compartment and the train left the station, but it was doubtful if he would have felt so extremely pleased with himself if he had been aware of the identity of the man who was travelling in the next carriage. But he was not aware of this, and therefore his pleasure was unspoilt. Oh, undoubtedly he was clever, he thought complacently. His handling of the whole affair had been remarkably smart. The Grim Joker was clever, but he, Sellick, was cleverer. He had seized a chance that was going to make him independent for the rest of his life.

His mind was still filled with rose-coloured plans for the future when at his journey's end he raised his hand and gave the peculiar knock on Mr. Kyne's knocker. This time it was the stout money-lender himself who opened the door and ushered his visitor into the large ornately furnished room. There was an air of excitement and nervousness about the man that he could not conceal, and his smooth face glistened with little beads of perspiration.

'Well,' said the butler, smacking him on the back heartily, 'everything seems to be going fine.'

'I hope you're right,' retorted Mr. Kyne gloomily.

Sellick looked surprised. 'Why, what's the matter with you? Fifty thousand pounds as easy as kiss your hand and no trouble, isn't that fine?'

The fat man shook his head pessimistically. 'Sounds a little too easy to me,' he grunted. 'You want to be careful of this fellow, Sellick. He's a dangerous man. Remember those other people he's killed. Why shouldn't the same thing happen to us?'

The butler laughed harshly. 'Nonsense!' he exclaimed. 'He daren't try any funny business. He wouldn't have written to you making the appointment if he was going to try to double-cross us. I told him after the murder that if he didn't make this appointment, I'd split to the police. There's nothing to worry about.'

Mr. Kyne wiped his shining face. 'Well, I hope you're right,' he said, and opening a drawer in the writing table he took out a sheet of paper and passed it over to the other. 'There's the letter,' he went on. 'He wants you to meet him at twelve o'clock tonight in Quarry Wood. There's a place where they've been cutting down trees. He's put full directions for finding it.'

'I can read that for myself,' snarled Sellick, and Mr. Kyne lapsed into silence.

The butler read the letter twice; then, folding it, he put it in his pocket. 'You'd better take me within walking distance of the place in your car,' he said, 'and then wait to bring me back. I oughtn't be more than an hour at the outside. If I'm not back by that time, you can go to the nearest police station and tell all you know.'

Mr. Kyne agreed reluctantly, and they sat talking until the chiming of the clock in the hall warned them that it was time to be moving. The smooth man went out into the lobby and struggled into his coat. His car was garaged less than a hundred yards from the flat in which he lived, and in a few seconds they were speeding in the big saloon *en route* for Quarry Wood.

Sellick drove, and once clear of the traffic he let the car out, and in an incredibly short space of time they were on the Bath Road and running towards Slough. It was barely twenty minutes to twelve when they passed through Maidenhead and swung to the right and on up the hill leading to Quarry Wood. The butler turned off into a side turning and brought the car to a stop.

'I'll walk from here,' he said; and Mr. Kyne, huddled up in his seat, nodded.

The night was very dark, and it looked as if it was gathering up to rain, for the pale moon that had been in evidence when they had left the West End was no longer visible. Leaving Kyne in the car, Sellick crossed a strip of grass and plunged among the trees. He was filled with pleasurable anticipation; for, throughout his career as sneak-thief, burglar and blackmailer, he had always had visions of something really big, a tremendous coup that would allow him to live in luxury for the rest of his life. That he had not got the brains to plan it never occurred to him. Like all crooks, he was inordinately vain and mistook a certain low cunning, which he did possess, for something appertaining to genius. The prisons are full of people like Sellick who think the same, and continue to think so even after they have been caught.

He reached the wood and entered the straggling fringe of trees. The place was silent and deserted, and he found it difficult in the darkness to follow the directions contained in the letter. Presently, however, he came upon the place which the Grim Joker had mentioned: a little clearing in which a number of trees had been felled.

There was no sign of the man he was going to meet, and he walked up and down impatiently. He heard a clock somewhere in the distance strike twelve, and peered about him, but the gloomy wood was silent and deserted. Leaning up against the trunk of a tree, he lit a cigarette and smoked, cursing softly.

A long interval went by, and still nobody came. The excitement that had filled him was wearing off, and for the first time he experienced a little qualm of fear. Supposing this man should serve him as he had served his other victims?

He shivered, and then the thought of the stout Mr. Kyne waiting close at hand gave him courage. The Grim Joker, for his own sake, dare not harm him, for he knew that the money-lender shared his secret, and that if anything happened to Sellick he would instantly communicate with the police. At the same time, it was unpleasant in this dark and silent wood, and if anything should happen Mr. Kyne was too far away to render assistance. It wouldn't do Sellick much good to know that his death would be avenged.

Presently as the time went on, his fear gave place to anger. If this fellow thought he could treat him like this, he would show him. Twelve o'clock had been the time, and now it must be nearly half-past. He'd tell him a few things when he did come.

Suddenly he heard a sound, and listening, discovered it to be approaching footsteps. Out of the darkness loomed a figure, and he uttered a sigh of relief. The newcomer drew nearer, came to within a yard of where Sellick was standing, and halted.

'Is that you?' asked a voice sharply.

'It's me,' answered the butler.

'Well then, let's get to business as quickly as possible,' said the other, 'for I've got a lot to do.'

'Well, you know what I want,' said Sellick, forgetting in his cupidity to grumble at the other for his lateness. 'Fifty thousand, and I'll keep quiet.'

'Blackmail, eh?' said the Grim Joker softly.

'You can call it that if you like,' growled Sellick, 'or you can call it a little present. I don't care so long as you hand over the cash.'

The man he addressed smiled, but the smile was not good to see. 'You don't suppose I've brought it with me, do you?' he asked.

The butler eyed him suspiciously.

'What do you mean?' he said. 'You promised — '

'I promised that I'd pay you well for keeping your mouth shut, and I'm prepared to keep my promise. But you can't have the money yet. Until I've completed this business, I haven't got it.'

'You can give me some of it,' growled Sellick. 'I don't mind if it's only five thousand on account.'

'I can't give you a penny,' said the other impatiently. 'It'll be several weeks before I can draw any money, and you'll have to wait till then.'

An ugly expression crossed the butler's face. 'Oh, will I?' he snarled. 'Who do you think you're talking to, eh? I'm the fellow to dictate terms. You'll either hand me over five thousand on account by tomorrow night, or I'll go straight away to the police and spill the beans.'

'That would be a foolish thing to do, my friend. Your trouble is greediness, Sellick. If you go to the police, you get nothing. If you wait for a week or two, you get fifty thousand.'

'Do I?' snapped the butler. 'What

guarantee have I got for that? By that time you may have slipped out of the country.'

'You'll have to take my word,' said the other shortly.

'Oh yes,' sneered Sellick. 'What do you take me for, a mug, eh? I'll tell you what I'll do. You bring five thousand pounds here at the same time tomorrow night, and I'll wait for the balance for a month. You can't bluff me with all that nonsense about not having any money. I'll bet you've got some put away, and I want it, see?'

'I see,' said the Grim Joker; and his right hand, which had been in the pocket of his overcoat throughout the interview, moved quickly. There was a flash and a dull plop, like the drawing of a cork.

The scream which rose in Sellick's throat died. For a second he swayed back and forth, glaring at the man who had sent a bullet through his heart with a dreadful fixed stare, and then he slowly crumpled into a heap and lay still.

The killer replaced the still-smoking pistol, with its attached silencer, in his pocket, and bent over the huddled form. Jerking open the coat, he felt for the heart.

'Quite dead,' he muttered calmly.

Straightening up, he listened for a moment, glanced quickly about him, and then walked rapidly away in the direction whence he had come.

18

Mr. Kyne Is Scared

Mr. Oswald Kyne, dozing in his car, knew nothing of the tragedy that had taken place so near to him. Although he had agreed to Sellick's suggestion that if he was not back in an hour he would inform the police of what they knew, he had never had any intention of doing it. Mr. Kyne was not in the least anxious to bring himself before the notice of the law. His whole life had been spent in avoiding contact with the police, and he had no wish that this state of affairs should be altered.

It was all very well to threaten the man they were blackmailing that unless he paid up, they would inform the police of his identity; but it was quite another matter to do so, at least personally. A carefully written anonymous letter was feasible, but anything else would be sheer madness.

With a half-smoked cigar between his lips, Mr. Kyne sat patiently, his chin sunk on his breast, waiting for the return of his associate. The time passed slowly. Twice he switched on the light on the dashboard and looked at the clock, discovering rather to his surprise that less than three-quarters of an hour had elapsed since Sellick had left him. Presently he heard a clock strike one, and moved impatiently. He was tired, and although the car was comfortable he preferred the greater comfort of his flat. Mr. Kyne led a well-ordered life. He was in the habit of retiring to bed punctually at half-past eleven, and this upsetting of his habits disturbed him.

When another quarter of an hour had dragged itself slowly by, he began to feel uneasy. Surely it was time Sellick was back by now? He had been gone an hour and a quarter — ample time to conclude the interview.

A sudden idea occurred to Mr. Kyne. Supposing Sellick had double-crossed him? Supposing he had received the fifty thousand pounds he had demanded from the Grim Joker and made off with it?

He took the cigar from between his teeth and flung it through the open window into the roadway. It was curious the possibility had never occurred to him before. It was not because he had any illusions concerning Sellick's character, but because he was so used to being in the position of dictator that the thought had never crossed his mind. And yet there was no reason why Sellick should return with the money. There was, in fact, every reason why he should not. Twenty-five thousand perfectly good reasons. If he had succeeded in extracting the fifty thousand from the man he had gone to meet, it was more than likely he had planned to clear off with the lot instead of coming back and sharing it with Mr. Kyne.

The expression on that gentleman's smooth face was not pleasant as he became more and more convinced that this was what had happened. Sellick would know that he was helpless to do anything. He couldn't give the man away without bringing himself into the business, and the sleek-haired butler knew him well enough to be sure that that was the last thing he would do.

Another quarter of an hour went by, and Mr. Kyne became filled with a cold rage. Sellick had used him to further his plans, and now that they had matured had thrown him aside like a burnt match. He was trembling with fury as he got out of the car and approached the wood.

His anger had destroyed all his previous premonitions of danger. There was just the possible chance that the man had not turned up and that Sellick was still waiting at the meeting place. Mr. Kyne determined to find out. He had memorised the directions contained in the letter for finding the spot, and began carefully -to pick his way through the darkness of the wood towards it.

He came upon the little clearing with the felled trees and stopped, listening. There was no sound of life and no sign of any living presence. With a muttered oath, he advanced. His idea had been right — Sellick had done him down. And then his foot kicked something, something that was too soft to be a log . . .

He felt the perspiration start out on his forehead and fumbled in his pocket for his matches. With difficulty, he struck one.

The next instant he was stumbling blindly back the way he had come, towards his car, his eyes staring and his breath whistling irregularly between his parted lips.

Sellick had not double-crossed him. That horror amid the bracken had been Sellick. His premonition had been realised.

He reached the car panting and dizzy, for he was not used to strenuous exercise. So spent was he that he had to clutch at the window frame for support and lean against the body to recover his breath. Before his eyes he could still see that white, agonised face and the wet patch on the front of the coat. He was attacked by a violent shivering. His skin felt clammy and damp, and the perspiration stood out on his face in little beads.

Presently he recovered himself sufficiently to climb shakily into the car. He must get away from this spot as quickly as possible. The murderer might still be lurking about somewhere in the silence and darkness of the night, and he had shared Sellick's secret. He was as much a danger to the Grim Joker as Sellick himself.

Although it was many years since he had driven, he started the engine and fumbled with the gears. The car moved forward, and with difficulty he managed to turn it. A sigh of relief escaped his lips as he left the turning by Quarry Wood and began to drive slowly and clumsily back towards London.

It was half-past three when he brought the car to his garage. Handing it over to the night man, he walked the short distance to his flat. As he closed his front door behind him, the terror that had accompanied him throughout his journey abated somewhat. In the midst of the familiar appointments of his flat he felt more at ease.

Removing his hat and coat, he went

into his study and poured himself out a stiff drink. The spirit took effect, and as he lit a cigar and sank into the chair behind his desk he felt almost his normal self. He was desperately tired, but no thought of bed entered his head. There was a lot to think about, and he wanted to straighten his disordered thoughts.

Sellick's attempt at blackmail had failed, and Sellick had paid the penalty for his temerity. Well, he had been warned. It was his fault that he had taken no notice. What he, Kyne, had suggested might happen, *had* happened.

Gradually, as the whisky restored his nerve and the fragrant cigar soothed his senses, Mr. Kyne began to look upon the happenings of the night from a different angle.

Perhaps it was a good job that Sellick was out of the way. Perhaps there was a possibility that he could turn the killing to profit himself. He knew what Sellick had known, and in his case there would be no one to split the fifty thousand pounds with.

Fifty thousand pounds! His smooth

face creased into a smile. Perhaps it wouldn't rest at that. Perhaps this Grim Joker man could be induced to part with more.

Mr. Kyne wished that he knew what lay behind it all. Except that he was aware of the identity of the Grim Joker, he knew nothing. The reason for the killing of Hamilton Lorne, Percival Haynes and the others was a complete mystery to him. Sellick had not troubled to find that out, and that was one of the mistakes he had made. He had contented himself with knowing the Joker's identity. If the object of the murders was money, then Mr. Kyne wanted to know how much was involved, so that he could cut in and take his share.

Fifty thousand pounds was quite a respectable sum, but a hundred thousand was even better, and two hundred thousand better than that.

That in meddling with this man he was incurring considerable danger, he knew, but the cupidity at the root of his nature overruled his fear. Sellick had bungled the whole affair. He had gone at it like a bull at a gate. It required handling much more subtly, and Mr. Kyne prided himself on possessing the necessary qualifications.

There was one stumbling block he could not for the moment see a way of surmounting, and that was that he had no idea how to get in touch with the Grim Joker. Sellick had made the man promise to write and fix an appointment when he had witnessed the murder at Dorking, and the Grim Joker had kept his promise — with disastrous results to Sellick. But so far as Mr. Kyne was concerned, his present whereabouts were unknown.

He laid the stump of his cigar in his ashtray and carefully lit another. There must be some way of getting round this.

The sun was flooding the streets with golden light when he finally hit on a plan. It required working out in detail, but it was certainly a possible solution to his difficulties.

Rising wearily to his feet, he stretched himself. He had done enough thinking for one session. His brain was tired, and a spell of sleep would sharpen his wits and enable him to perfect the scheme that had suggested itself.

He wrote a note to his housemaid instructing her that he was not to be disturbed, and attaching this with a drawing-pin to his bedroom door, locked himself in and undressing, quickly slipped into bed.

His head had barely touched the pillow before he was asleep, and he slept dreamlessly until late in the afternoon, when he awoke to receive the first of the succession of shocks that were to shake him to the very foundations of his life.

19

Sergeant Leek Gets Reprimanded

Sergeant Leek came into Mr. Budd's office, a worried frown on his long face and his manner a little more nervous and apologetic than usual.

The stout man, who was glowering at a heap of papers in front of him, looked up. 'Good mornin',' he said. 'You look full of the joy of spring. What's the matter?'

'It's about that feller, Sellick,' Leek began uneasily.

Mr. Budd pushed aside his papers and leaned back in his chair. 'Well, what about him?' he asked.

'You know we was 'avin' 'im watched,' answered the sergeant. 'Well, Davis lost him last night. Sellick gave 'im the slip at Piccadilly Circus.'

Mr. Budd's brows drew together in a portentous frown. 'Oh, he did, did he?' he murmured ominously. 'That feller Davis must be a bright lad. He didn't lose himself by any chance, did he?'

'I don't think it was Davis's fault,' said the miserable Leek. 'I've always found him a very reliable chap — '

'Your idea of reliability and mine don't agree,' broke in the superintendent crossly. 'If this feller Davis was reliable, he wouldn't have lost his man. It was very important that Sellick should be watched, an' I left you to attend to it. Naturally I thought you'd put on men who knew their job, not nitwits.'

He picked up the telephone receiver as the bell rang. 'Hello!' he growled, and then after a short interval: 'Put her through, will you?'

Sergeant Leek welcomed the interruption. He hoped that by the time Mr. Budd returned to the subject of Davis, he would be in a more amenable frame of mind, but in this he was to be disappointed. After a long conversation with the person at the other end of the wire, Mr. Budd hung up the receiver and turned to his subordinate.

'That was Miss Grayson, as I've no

doubt you've guessed,' he said. 'Yesterday was Sellick's afternoon off an' he left the house shortly after tea. He hasn't yet come back. So you see what your reliable fellow Davis has let us in for. It looks to me as though Sellick has cleared out for good. If we'd known where he went to last night, we might have learned a lot.' He little knew how much truth there was in what he said.

'I'm very sorry,' muttered the unhappy Leek.

'And so you ought to be,' said Mr. Budd severely. 'I left this Sellick business in your hands and you go and mess it up.'

An idea occurred to the sergeant and he put it forward eagerly. 'Perhaps this fellow Sellick went to see Kyne again,' he suggested.

'Most probably he did,' grunted Mr. Budd, 'but I don't suppose he stopped there all night. It's where he is at present that I want to know.'

He was not to be left long in doubt, for he had scarcely finished speaking when the telephone rang again. Leek saw his superior's face change as he listened to the message that came over the wire, and from Mr. Budd's conversation was prepared for the news that lethargic man had to tell him.

'Sellick was found at ten o'clock this mornin' shot dead in Quarry Wood, between Maidenhead and Marlow,' he said as he banged the telephone back on its rest. 'The body was found by some boys who had gone into the woods to play. You're partly responsible for the death of this feller, Leek. If Davis hadn't lost him last night, it might have been prevented.'

The sergeant took no notice of this outrageous charge. 'I wonder what he was doing in Quarry Wood,' he said, knitting his brows.

'He wasn't pickin' wildflowers,' said Mr. Budd. 'And he wasn't shot by a sparrow, like the feller in the fairytale. Go and order a car. I'm goin' down to see the body. And see that Davis isn't drivin',' he added darkly as Leek turned to obey, 'otherwise instead of gettin' to Quarry Wood we shall find ourselves on Hilly Fields.'

He was silent during the journey, much to the relief of the sergeant, and said very little when he viewed the remains of Sellick in the little mortuary at Maidenhead. The contents of the butler's pockets had been piled on a little table beside the slab on which his body lay, and the superintendent inspected these. There was nothing of interest except a letter written on cheap paper in the same spidery, childish handwriting that was a characteristic of the communications from the Grim Joker.

Mr. Budd read it and frowned. 'There's no doubt this Jokin' fellow was the murderer,' he said. 'This letter was makin' an appointment to meet Sellick in Quarry Wood last night at twelve o'clock. That means there was a connection between Sellick and the Grim Joker. I thought there might be somethin' of the sort.' He looked at Leek and shook his head sadly. 'We lost a wonderful chance of gettin' that fellow last night,' he said. 'You an' that fellow Davis have got a lot to answer for.'

It was the finding of the letter which

had caused the county police to ring up Scotland Yard. A specimen of the Grim Joker's writing had been forwarded months before to every police station in the country, and when the letter had been found in Sellick's pocket the inspector-in-charge had recognised the writing and immediately communicated with police headquarters.

Mr. Budd took charge of the letter, and when he had discovered from the local police the exact conditions under which Sellick had been found, returned to town. He seldom ate lunch when he was busy, contenting himself with sandwiches and coffee. When these had been sent in to him and he had slowly consumed the last crumb and the last drop, he sent for Leek.

'Now listen,' he said. 'I want to find a feller who may be a crook known to the police, or maybe not. I don't know his name, but I'll give you a general description of him. He's either recently been to a dentist and had all his teeth out, or has undergone that operation some time durin' his life. You won't be able to

184

pull the feller in because I believe you'll find he's missin'. But get busy on it — and don't employ that feller Davis.'

The sergeant took his departure to set in motion enquiries for the man his superior was searching for, and he went greatly puzzled, for he hadn't the least idea what was in the back of Mr. Budd's mind or why he wished to discover the whereabouts of this toothless individual.

At half-past three that afternoon, the stout superintendent put on his hat and, leaving the Yard, hailed a taxi and was driven to the block of flats in which Mr. Oswald Kyne had his luxurious abode. He squeezed himself with difficulty into the little lift, and stepping out at the fourth floor knocked on the door of Mr. Kyne's flat. His summons was answered by the sullen-faced maid.

'I want to see Mr. Oswald Kyne,' said Mr. Budd genially, in reply to her curt question. 'Take him my card, will you?' He fished in his waistcoat pocket and produced an official card, which he handed to the woman. As she looked at it, he saw her face change. Its surliness gave way to an expression of apprehension.

'I don't know whether Mr. Kyne is in,' she said a little huskily. 'I'll see.'

She closed the door and Mr. Budd waited. He waited for a considerable time before she returned and, opening the door, ushered him into the hall. 'Will you come this way, please,' she said, and going across to the study door, held it open.

The Rosebud entered and was greeted by the smooth-faced Mr. Kyne, who was sitting at his desk clad in a varied-hued silk dressing-gown, which he had obviously hastily assumed over his pyjamas. The sleepy eyes of the stout man took in the expensive furnishings as he advanced slowly into the room.

'Good afternoon, er, Superintendent,' said Mr. Kyne, glancing at the card which he held between his smooth fingers. 'To what am I indebted for this visit?' Behind the jovial exterior of the man, Mr. Budd sensed a certain uneasiness.

'I've come to make some enquiries concernin' a man called Sellick,' he said slowly. 'I believe you knew him?'

There was a momentary pause before

Mr. Kyne shook his head. 'I'm afraid your information is wrong,' he answered. 'I know no one of the name of Sellick.'

'That's very extraordinary,' said Mr. Budd, raising his eyebrows. 'Very extraordinary indeed. He was seen to call here the night before last.'

The smooth man hastily corrected himself. 'Oh, now I think I know who you are talking about,' he said. 'I have a lot of callers, er, Superintendent, and I can't remember them all, naturally. Now I come to think of it, however, I do remember this man you're talking about. He was in the employ of that poor fellow Dr. Roone, wasn't he?'

The Rosebud inclined his head. 'That's right.'

'Yes, I remember now,' went on Mr. Kyne. 'He called to see me with reference to a situation. He had apparently heard, quite erroneously, that I was in need of a manservant, and the tragic death of his employer having left him, er, disengaged, he called to see if I would take him on.'

'And it took you nearly an hour and a half to decide,' murmured the big man.

'We were talking about the murder most of the time,' explained Mr. Kyne frankly. 'I had been reading an account of it in the evening newspapers, and naturally was interested in hearing any details at first hand, as you might say.'

'Naturally. So that's all you know about Sellick?'

'That's all I know about him.'

'He didn't call to see you last night, by any chance?'

For a moment Mr. Kyne was undecided what to say. Was this another trap? Had Sellick been followed to his flat on the previous night as he had, apparently, on the occasion before? He had to make up his mind quickly and he decided to risk it.

'No,' he said. 'The time you mentioned is the only time he's been here.'

Mr. Budd had noticed the slight hesitation before he had answered the question and formed his own conclusions. There was little doubt in his own mind that Sellick had visited this man on the night when he had kept his appointment with the Grim Joker in

Quarry Wood, but owing to the failure of Davis he had no proof of this. Outwardly, at any rate, he was therefore forced to accept Mr. Kyne's word.

'May I ask why you are making these enquiries, Officer?' said that gentleman. 'I hope that this man Sellick was not, er, a criminal?'

'Why do you say 'was'?' said Mr. Budd gently. 'Anyone'd think you knew he was dead.'

Mr. Kyne cursed himself for the slip. 'Dead!' he exclaimed. 'Good gracious me! How — how dreadful! When did he die?'

'Accordin' to the police doctor, it was shortly after one this mornin'. He was shot dead in Quarry Wood.'

'Murdered!' Mr. Kyne's flaccid face was twisted into a very good imitation of surprise.

'He was murdered by this feller they call the Grim Joker,' Mr. Budd added.

The face of the man before him was horrified. 'Dear me! Was he mixed up with that dreadful man?' he cried. 'You astonish me, Superintendent.'

'I've astonished a good many people in

my time,' remarked the Rosebud thoughtfully. He looked sleepily at Mr. Kyne's sketchy attire. 'Just got up?' he asked.

The smooth man was disconcerted. 'Er, yes. I — I haven't been feeling very well today.'

'I see. I thought perhaps it might have been because you didn't get to bed last night.'

Mr. Kyne laughed, not very successfully. 'I'm not young enough to stay up all night. As a matter of fact, I went to bed quite early.'

'Early to bed is good for the nerves,' said Mr. Budd, and he rose a little wearily to his feet. 'Well, I'm sorry you can't give me any more information. I was hopin' you knew more about this fellow Sellick.'

'I'm sorry I don't, for your sake,' said Mr. Kyne, 'and very glad for my own. Naturally, I don't want to be mixed up with this sort of person.'

'Naturally,' agreed Mr. Budd, and he took his leave, quite satisfied with the result of his interview.

Immediately he had gone, Mr. Oswald Kyne pulled the telephone towards him and gave a number.

'Is that Walker's Garage?' he said when he was connected. 'Is that you, George? This is Mr. Kyne speaking. Listen! If there are any enquiries as to whether my car was out last night, it wasn't. You understand?'

They evidently did understand, for he hung up the receiver with a sigh of relief. He was a good payer, and he knew that if the police made any enquiries at Walker's Garage they would receive no information.

His relief in the circumstances was premature, but he did not know this, for a constable on point duty had seen and recognised the car when it came back at half-past three in the morning and remembered this fact when later he was questioned by his superiors.

20

The People at the Cottage

Mr. Budd went back to the Yard and employed the half-hour following his arrival in his office by issuing a string of instructions to various departments. When he had finished these, he leaned back in his chair and lit one of his inevitable black cigars.

He had done all that was necessary concerning Mr. Kyne. The Sellick end of the case, in his opinion, was not very important. He guessed how the dead man had come into the business, for when he had told Larry that he knew the identity of the Grim Joker he had spoken no more than the truth. His trouble at the moment was that he had insufficient evidence to bring before a jury, apart from which a premature move might result in the man slipping through his fingers for good and all. He was, however, fairly satisfied with the progress he was making. The reports that had come in that morning, prior to the discovery of Sellick's murder, had pleased him and cleared up several points on which he had been rather vague.

He sat motionless in his usual position for nearly an hour, and then rousing himself from his thoughts he left his office, went downstairs, and passing out of the building, sought among the parked vehicles in the quadrangle for his own dilapidated little car. Squeezing himself with difficulty behind the wheel, he drove out through the Whitehall entrance and headed for Dorking. He arrived at Larry's house at a little after seven, to the surprise of its owner.

'Hello!' said Larry as the big man ambled into the dining-room, where he was having his dinner. 'How did you manage to summon up sufficient energy to get down here?'

Mr. Budd ignored the insult. 'Thought I'd like to look you up and talk about this fellow you met in the wood,' he said, dropping into a chair. 'If you'd like to offer me somethin' to eat and a glass of beer, I won't say no, but don't bother.'

Larry grinned and rang the bell. When Mrs. Clipp had brought an appetising plate of cold beef and salad and a large bottle of beer, and Mr. Budd was seated opposite his host and sampling both, Larry continued the conversation.

'I've told you all I know about the man,' he said, 'and that's nothing. I've had the police up here interviewing me, and they've been making enquiries in the neighbourhood, but I don't think they've discovered anything. By the way, I suppose you know that Sellick has vanished.'

Mr. Budd swallowed half a glass of beer at a gulp. 'Yes, I know that,' he said. 'And he won't reappear. He was killed early this mornin' in a wood near Maidenhead.' He told his astonished and interested friend what had happened to the unfortunate butler.

'Good Lord!' said Larry. 'Does Miss Grayson know about this?'

'I don't think so. I thought we'd go over together and break the news. There's plenty of time,' Mr. Budd added as Larry half-rose. 'I can appreciate how glad you are of an excuse, but I've had nothin' all day except a few sandwiches, and I'd like to finish my dinner first.'

Larry reddened. 'I was only going to get some more bread,' he said crossly, and going to the sideboard he cut himself a piece from the loaf.

'Oh, I'm sorry,' murmured the stout man. 'I thought you was thinkin' of dashin' off straight away to the Larches.' There was a twinkle in his eye as he looked at his friend innocently.

'You thought nothing of the sort,' said Larry. 'You were just trying to take a rise out of me.'

Dusk was creeping down when they left the house and set off on their visit. Larry wanted to take the short cut through the wood and along the lane that bisected the fields, but Mr. Budd apparently preferred to go round by way of the road.

'It's much longer,' protested Larry, 'and you know you hate exercise.'

'A walk after a meal is very beneficial,' said the stout man surprisingly. 'I've been thinkin' for a long time that I don't get enough walkin'.'

'I'm glad to hear it,' said Larry.

They came out of the drive on to the narrow country road and turned in the direction that would bring them to the Larches. On their left lay the wheat field where the Grim Joker had played his supreme joke, but the scarecrow no longer fluttered its tattered garments in the breeze.

They reached the entrance to Roone's house, and Larry was turning into the wide gateway when the superintendent stopped him. 'What's that place over there?' he asked, and pointed towards the low roof of a cottage half-hidden by the trees that grew thickly round it.

'That's Whitegate,' said Larry. 'It's only recently been let. I don't know who the people are. If you remember, poor Roone mentioned it that day at my place.'

Mr. Budd nodded slowly. He did remember it. He also remembered the effect the apparently innocuous statement had had on Norma Grayson. 'You don't know who the people are?' he murmured.

Larry shook his head. 'No, I've never seen them.'

Mr. Budd said no more, but his brows were drawn together as he followed his friend up the drive to the main entrance.

Here they received a disappointment. The maid who opened the door informed them that her mistress had just gone out. 'I don't know how long she'll be, either, sir,' she volunteered. 'She said she was going for a walk. Would you care to come in and wait?'

'We'll call back later,' said the superintendent before Larry could reply. 'It's a beautiful evenin', and I think it'd do us good if we followed Miss Grayson's example.' The maid smiled and closed the door.

'I don't know what's come over you,' said Larry as they turned away. 'What's the reason for this great display of energy?'

'Nature always affects me like that,' replied Mr. Budd untruthfully. 'If I lived in the country, I should probably become as thin as you are.'

Larry grunted unbelievingly. 'There's

something behind your suggestion of a walk,' he said. 'Unless you had a reason, you wouldn't walk a step.'

'Maybe you're right,' said the superintendent. 'As a matter of fact, you *are* right. To be perfectly candid, I'm rather interested in that cottage we was talkin' about just now.'

Larry looked at him in astonishment. 'What on earth for?'

'Call it a hunch. I just feel that it'd be worth lookin' at. I suppose there's some way of gettin' at it?'

'There's a lane that runs past the gate.'

'Then we'll walk along that way,' murmured the stout man. He felt in his pocket and produced a cigar. 'No good offerin' you one of these,' he said. 'You don't like 'em.'

When it was alight and he had drawn one or two preliminary puffs, he went on: 'Do you remember, just as we was leavin' on the mornin' Roone was killed, a burly-lookin' feller callin' to see Miss Grayson?'

Larry, who until that moment had forgotten the incident, started. 'Yes, I do,' he answered. 'Why?'

'I'm wonderin',' said Mr. Budd thoughtfully, 'whether his visit had anythin' to do with this wild man you met in the wood. I don't know whether you heard what the feller said as he was goin' upstairs, but if you didn't I did, and directly you mentioned this man with the knife I sort of connected the two.'

'Yes, I heard what he said. Something about somebody having escaped.'

Mr. Budd nodded. 'That's right.'

'But what have the people at Whitegate got to do with it?'

'I don't know that they've got anythin' to do with it, but I've got an idea that they're associated in some way with Miss Grayson; and since this prize-fightin' feller is also associated with her, it looks to me as if they might have a lot to do with it.' He told his friend of the agitation with which Norma had received Doctor Roone's remark that the cottage was let.

'I didn't notice it,' said Larry.

'It was one of the few times you weren't lookin' at her!'

They were strolling along the narrow lane, which was so narrow that the hedges on either side rubbed their shoulders. Larry was thoughtful and a little worried. What could Norma Grayson have to do with the lunatic-man with the knife who had screamed at him in the wood?

It suddenly occurred to him that anyway it was her secret, and they had little right to pry into her private affairs. He mentioned this to Mr. Budd, but that lethargic man was not in agreement.

'That's all very heroic and romantic,' he said, 'but I'm investigatin' a series of murders. Fine feelin's are all very well, but you can't let 'em stand in the way of gettin' at the truth.'

'But Miss Grayson's got nothing to do with the murders!' exclaimed Larry hotly.

'I'm not sayin' she has, not at any rate directly. But indirectly, she may have a lot to do with 'em. These people at the cottage may have got her in their power. I know that sounds like somethin' out of a novel, but you'd be surprised how often I've come across things that are just like bits from a book. They may be blackmailin' her, in which case we'll be doin' her a good turn if we find out all about it.'

Larry was still a little dubious in spite of this argument. However, he said no more; and presently, rounding a sharp turn in the little lane, they came in sight of the cottage gate. Originally it may have been white and so given to the place its name, but time and weather had reduced its pristine glory to a drab and indeterminate shade of grey.

As they drew near, they heard the sound of voices, and drawing level with the gate saw whence they came. Three people were standing in the small garden in front of the cottage talking earnestly together. One was the thick-set man with the ugly face, and the other two consisted of a thin grey-haired woman and Norma Grayson. The latter turned as she heard their footsteps, and Mr. Budd stopped.

'Good evenin', Miss Grayson,' he said pleasantly. 'It's a lovely evenin', isn't it?'

She stared at him in silence, and Larry saw with a sinking heart that there was stark fear in her eyes.

21

Mr. Clipp Breaks His Rule

With an effort, Norma recovered from the shock caused by their sudden appearance and smiled faintly. 'It's lovely, isn't it?' she said. 'It was much too nice to stay indoors, so I came out for a walk.'

'We thought the same,' said Mr. Budd conversationally. 'We thought we might run into this wild feller who's loose in the neighbourhood.'

The fear that was still lurking in Norma's eyes deepened, and she shot a quick glance at her two companions. 'What — what man is this?' she asked in a low voice.

'Mr. Weston knows more about him than I do,' replied the stout man. 'Apparently he's a feller who's roamin' the countryside with a knife. He attacked Mr. Weston the other night in the little wood near his house.'

Something akin to horror appeared in her face as she turned to Larry. 'Is — is that true?' she asked tremulously.

'Yes,' Larry answered. 'I didn't tell you because I didn't want to frighten you. I notified the police and they've been looking for him.'

'What was he like?' said Norma, and Larry gave her a brief description.

'Sounds like a tramp,' put in the thick-set man who had not spoken before. 'Probably he's miles away by now.'

'Maybe you're right,' Mr. Budd said. 'All the same, he seems a dangerous feller. You want to be careful, Miss Grayson, when you take these solitary walks.'

'I'm not afraid,' she answered. 'There's no reason why he should harm me.'

She was ill at ease and nervous. Larry concluded that their surprising her in conversation with the people at the cottage had disconcerted her.

Mr. Budd, who must have noticed her embarrassment, appeared oblivious to it. Glancing round the little garden, gay with flowers, he turned to the ugly-faced man.

'Nice place you've got here, Mr. — ' He paused suggestively, but that individual remained silent, refusing to supply the name the superintendent was obviously waiting for. 'Very nice little place,' he went on. 'Those roses want prunin' another year, an' you'll get more and better blooms. And there's a lot of dead wood on that rambler that could do with takin' away. You haven't been here very long, have you?'

Since it was difficult to avoid answering a direct question, the thick-set man shook his head. 'No,' he replied shortly.

'Well, you can't do much now,' continued Mr. Budd. 'But in another year, if you're thinkin' of stoppin', you ought to be able to make this garden beautiful.' He sighed and shook his head sadly. 'I wish I'd got a bit of ground like this,' he said enviously. 'It's the settin' that makes all the difference to a garden. You've got a natural settin' here which I haven't. My bit of ground's bordered by wooden fences. It's surprisin' what a few trees and a patch of shrubbery'll do to throw up the colour of the blooms.'

Apparently he had forgotten everything else except his hobby, for he continued to ramble on until Larry, who was getting a little impatient, stopped him. 'Don't you think we'd better be making a move?' he suggested, more on Norma's account than his own; and she must have sensed this, for she gave him a grateful glance.

'Have I been lettin' me tongue run away with me?' said Mr. Budd humorously. 'Well, well, once I get on the subject of gardens there's no stoppin' me. I hope I haven't been borin' you people?'

Nobody made the conventional denial, and the stout man's eyes twinkled.

'Apparently I have,' he murmured. 'Are you comin', Miss Grayson? There's one or two things I'd like to talk to you about.'

She looked a little apprehensive, but nodded. 'Yes, I'll come with you,' she answered. They said good night to the thin woman and the ugly-faced man and began to stroll down the lane in the direction of the Larches.

'That's the sort of place I'd like when I retire,' said Mr. Budd. 'It could be made very pretty with a little trouble. D'you know those people, Miss Grayson?'

She hesitated for a fraction of a second, then shook her head. 'No,' she answered. 'They were in the garden as I passed the gate, and — and they wished me good evening.'

'That's what I like about the country,' remarked the stout man. 'There's no stupid conventionality about it. People talk to one another without waitin' for introductions, an' everybody's friendly. That's as it should be. Now in London, if anybody wished you good evening that you didn't know, you'd imagine they was crooks, and in nine cases out of ten you'd be right.'

'Has — has anything been heard of Sellick?' asked Norma.

Larry thought the question had been prompted more with the object of diverting the conversation from the people at the cottage than from any very deep interest in the whereabouts of the butler.

'That's one of the things I wanted to talk to you about,' said Mr. Budd. 'As a

206

matter of fact we've found Sellick, and I think you ought to see about gettin' a new servant.'

'Do you mean he's in the hands of the police?' she asked sharply.

The superintendent nodded.

'Has he been arrested?'

'Well no, he hasn't exactly been arrested,' replied Mr. Budd, 'but he's in the hands of the police all the same. The inquest is bein' held the day after tomorrow.'

She caught her breath. 'Inquest? You mean — he's dead?'

'I'm afraid he is.'

'How did he die? Was it an accident?'

'No, it wasn't an accident,' said Mr. Budd. 'It was the furthest thing from an accident that I've ever seen.'

She guessed his meaning and her face went white. 'You're trying to tell me he was murdered! How — how dreadful! Who killed him?'

'The same feller who killed all these other people,' replied the superintendent. 'The man we call the Grim Joker.'

They had reached the drive gates of the

Larches and by common consent came to a halt. 'Won't you come in?' asked Norma, and her voice was a little tremulous. She had known very little of Sellick, and what she had known she had disliked, but it was a shock all the same to hear that the man had met with a violent death.

'Suppose you come along to my place?' suggested Larry, and she accepted his invitation almost eagerly. The house, with its atmosphere of tragedy, held no attraction for her, and she rather welcomed the possibility of a change, even for a brief period.

They continued along the narrow highway, and as they strolled along Mr. Budd gave Norma an account of the finding of Sellick's body in Quarry Wood. She listened with interest, and when he had finished put a question.

'I think he was killed because he knew the Grim Joker,' answered Mr. Budd. 'We found a letter on him, and I don't think there's much doubt he knew who the man was. He was tryin' a little blackmail, and he tried to blackmail the wrong person.'

They reached the house, and Larry took them into the pleasant drawing-room. When he had pushed forward a chair and seen that Norma was comfortable, he rang the bell and ordered Mrs. Clipp, who answered the summons, to make some coffee. The evening was warm and the windows were wide open. It was not yet quite dark, but the garden outside was bathed in the blue light of the approaching night.

'I wonder if you'll ever catch this man,' said Norma thoughtfully as Mr. Budd, after asking permission, lit one of his black cigars.

'I'm sure we shall catch him,' said the Rosebud confidently. 'And it's not goin' to be so very long now, either.'

'Did you mean what you said the other day?' said Larry. 'That you knew who he was?'

Mr. Budd nodded. 'I never say a thing unless I mean it,' he answered. 'At least, only now and again. Yes, I know who the Grim Joker is, an' I can pull him in just whenever I want to. At the moment I don't want to.'

Norma looked her surprise. 'You know him?' she asked incredulously.

'I've known him for several days,' said the superintendent. 'Now, Miss Grayson, I'm goin' to ask you one or two questions, and you mustn't get annoyed at what I'm goin' to say. Just forget for the moment that I'm a police officer, and look upon me as a friend.'

A troubled look came into her face, but she said nothing.

'A little while ago,' went on Mr. Budd, 'you pretended that you didn't know these people at that cottage, Whitegate. Now that wasn't quite true, was it?'

He waited for her to reply, but still she remained silent.

'You must know them pretty well,' he continued, 'because that feller came over to see you just as we was leavin' on the mornin' of the murder.'

She started.

'You'd forgotten that, hadn't you?' said Mr. Budd kindly. 'So you see, it's useless to continue to pretend that they're strangers.'

Her hands moved restlessly in her lap,

and she looked from the Rosebud to Larry uncomfortably. Larry shifted uneasily in his chair.

'Is it necessary to question Miss Grayson concerning her private affairs?' he muttered a little gruffly. 'Supposing she does know these people, is it any concern of ours?'

'It may not be of yours,' said Mr. Budd, 'but it is of mine. You've got somethin' worryin' you, Miss Grayson, and I think it would relieve your mind if you told us. As I said before, forget that I'm a detective.'

She moistened her lips.

'I'll admit that I do know these people,' she answered, 'but I'd rather not tell you anything else.'

'Tell me who this feller is?' persisted the Rosebud. 'This wild feller, who Mr. Weston met in the wood.'

There was a long period of silence.

'I'm sorry, but I can't tell you,' said the woman at last, and there was a touch of defiance in her voice. 'It's nobody's business but mine.'

'Well, if you won't, you won't,' Mr.

Budd sighed resignedly. 'I was hopin' you would, because it'd save a lot of trouble. I shall find out sooner or later, but I'd much rather you'd have told me, and so avoided the unpleasantness of a police enquiry.'

'I don't see why the police should come into it,' put in Larry angrily. 'Miss Grayson's quite right. It's nothing to do with anyone but herself.'

'When a feller who seems to be partially mad is allowed to wander about the countryside with a knife,' said Mr. Budd, 'it ceases to be a purely private matter and becomes a public one. Supposing this feller kills someone — what are you goin' to say then? That it's purely a private matter?'

'Oh, he won't,' said Norma. 'He wouldn't hurt anyone.'

Larry was silent. On this he found it difficult to agree with her, for the wild young man of the wood had seemed to him to be a pretty dangerous character.

Mr. Budd was just opening his lips to break the silence when he paused, the words unspoken, listening.

From outside had come a sound, the faint sound of an unmusical voice singing. Both Larry and Norma heard it, a shaky falsetto that was rapidly drawing nearer.

'It's a long way to Tipperary, it's a long way to go ... It's a long way to Tipperary, to the sweetest woman I know ...'

Larry uttered an angry exclamation. 'It's Clipp,' he said. 'He always sings when he's drunk!'

'Thought he only got drunk on Sundays?' remarked Mr. Budd.

'He's broken his rule,' snapped Larry.

The singing grew louder and more raucous as the singer came nearer the house, and now it was possible to distinguish another voice joining in the familiar refrain: 'Farewell Leicester Square ... It's a long way to Tipperary but my heart's right there.'

'Excuse me,' said Larry grimly; and pulling open the door, he went out into the hall.

Mr. Budd, his big face creasing into a smile, followed him, and after a moment's hesitation Norma joined them.

Larry jerked open the front door and, standing at the head of the steps, glared down the drive. Two unsteady figures came reeling towards him, arm in arm and singing lustily. And then, as the light from the hall light fell upon them, Larry gave a gasp of astonishment.

The smaller of the two was the undersized Mr. Clipp; and the other, whose arm he was grasping so affectionately, was the wild man of the wood!

22

The Attempt that Failed

Larry heard Norma's exclamation behind him and saw that she was staring with frightened eyes at Mr. Clipp's companion. With a reassuring word, he hurried down the steps and confronted his servant sternly.

'What do you mean by making all this row, Clipp?' he demanded. 'You ought to be ashamed of yourself.'

Mr. Clipp attempted to look dignified. 'Very shorry,' he said with difficulty. 'Jush having little cel'bration. Been made a colonel!'

'What the devil are you talking about?' snapped Larry angrily.

'Been made a colonel,' repeated Mr. Clipp thickly. 'Met my friend here, the field marshal, an' been made a colonel.'

'Tha's right,' said the wild man solemnly. 'Jolly good colonel. Make 'em all colonels. Only way to win the war, make 'em all colonels.'

The dumbfounded Larry stared at them, unable to think of anything to say.

'It's a grea' life,' mumbled Mr. Clipp, swaying backwards and forwards. 'A grea' life. Come, le's find the canteen.'

Larry found his voice. 'You've had enough of the canteen,' he said sternly. 'Go and put your head under the tap and get to bed. You're in a disgusting state!'

'Who are you?' demanded the wild man truculently. 'Don' know you an' don' want to know you.' His inflamed eyes regarded Larry suspiciously.

'Harry!' It was Norma's voice, curt and clear.

The man started, and his eyes narrowed. A cunning look crossed his face, and shaking himself free from the clutch of Mr. Clipp he swung round and began to run unsteadily down the drive. Norma flew past Larry and went after him. They saw her catch him up and grasp his arm. He turned with a snarl and aimed a blow at her that drew from her a little cry of pain.

Larry gritted his teeth and ran to her assistance. She was still holding on to the drunken man, and his arm was raised to hit her again, when Larry gripped him by the collar of his shirt and swung him round. 'That's enough of that!' he said savagely. 'You behave yourself!'

The man glared at him, his face distorted with passion. 'You let me alone,' he snarled, and struggled violently to free himself. 'I'll kill you if you interfere with me!'

His hand flew round to his hip pocket, but Larry, guessing he was searching for the knife he carried, gripped his wrist and twisted the arm up behind his back. A grunt of pain escaped the man's lips, but he was helpless.

'I think I'd better bring him back to the house,' said Larry gently to the white-faced Norma, and she nodded dumbly.

The man reeked of whisky, but although he was drunk he was by no means helpless, and fought and struggled every inch of the way as Larry propelled him up the drive. With the help of Mr. Budd, however, he succeeded in getting him into the house.

'I think it'd be safer if we tied him up,' murmured the stout man, and with a handkerchief and one of Larry's scarves they improvised shackles.

'What's happened to Clipp?' asked Larry when they had finished this task.

'He's passed out,' said Mr. Budd briefly. 'He's sleepin' peacefully under a rhododendron bush.'

Larry looked at Norma, and her troubled eyes met his. 'I'd better go and fetch Gill,' she said, and to his surprise her voice was quite calm.

'Is that the feller at the cottage?' asked Mr. Budd gently.

She nodded. 'Yes. His wife used to be my old nurse. They were looking after Harry, but he escaped.'

Mr. Budd glanced at the recumbent figure of the wild man, who seemed to have sunk into a stupor. 'Who is Harry?' he enquired.

'He's my brother,' answered Norma.

'I see,' said the stout man softly. 'How long has he been a dipsomaniac?'

'Ever since he was shell-shocked in the

war,' she replied. 'I've had a lot of trouble with him, but it really isn't his fault. He's all right as long as he can be kept away from drink. Mr. and Mrs. Gill have been very good. They've looked after him for years. It was at my suggestion they came down here.' Her voice broke slightly and she stopped.

'I'll go and fetch this fellow Gill,' said Mr. Budd. 'You stay here with Larry.'

He was gone before she could offer her thanks, and Larry led her gently into the drawing-room. 'You sit there,' he said, pulling forward a chair, 'and don't worry. I'll go and hurry Mrs. Clipp up with that coffee.'

He met the housekeeper in the hall, just about to bring in the tray. She was apologetic regarding her husband's lapse, but Larry cut short her flow. 'All right, I'll talk about it presently, Mrs. Clipp,' he said; and relieving her of the tray, he carried it back to the drawing-room.

Norma drank the coffee he poured out for her gratefully. 'I'm terribly sorry,' she said, 'that Harry should have made a disturbance here.'

'I don't think it was so much Harry's fault as my servant's,' said Larry. 'I wonder how they met?'

'I don't know. Harry escaped while Gill wasn't looking on the morning Dr. Roone was killed. Gill searched as much as he could, but he couldn't find him. I don't know where he's been hiding.'

'It must have been him who broke in here and stole my whisky,' said Larry with a chuckle.

'I guessed that when you mentioned it.' Norma was calmer, and the drawn look had gone from her face. Somehow the knowledge of this steady-looking man who was watching her sympathetically was very comforting. It seemed absurd now that she had not told him before.

He appeared to guess her thoughts, for his next remark was very applicable. 'Why didn't you tell me?' he said gently. 'I could have helped.'

'I was afraid to tell anyone,' she said. 'I didn't even tell Dr. Roone. I was afraid that they might want to shut Harry up, and he's such a dear when — when he's normal.'

'How often does he have these attacks?'

'Sometimes not for several months, but then the craving for drink gets too much for him and he'll go to any lengths to obtain it. It was only after he came back from the war that he got like this. I remember him when I was a child, and Mrs. Gill has told me since, that before then he never touched anything.'

'Have you had any opinion — medical opinion, I mean?'

'Not a proper one. Two ordinary doctors have seen him, and they wanted to call in a specialist, but his fees were too high. We couldn't afford it.'

'I have a friend who might be able to help you. I'll get him to come and examine your brother, if you like.'

'It's very good of you, Mr. Weston,' said Norma, 'but I couldn't think of allowing you to bother. There's no reason why you should worry yourself over my troubles.'

'I can tell you a very good one,' he said, and seeing the look in his eyes, she coloured. 'I'll go up and see Sir John Lannigan tomorrow,' he went on, mentioning the name of the finest nerve specialist in London. 'I'll get him to make an appointment to come and see your brother. I don't think you need worry about his having to be shut up. He may have to go into a nursing home, but there's nothing in that.'

She stared at him in dismay. 'But — the cost!' she protested.

'Never mind about it,' said Larry firmly. 'I'll attend to all that.' And then, as he saw her frown: 'I'll stop it out of your salary.'

They were still arguing about it when Mr. Budd returned with the ugly-faced Gill. The soporific effects of the drink he had consumed had overcome Harry Grayson and they had little difficulty in getting him back to the cottage.

'Well,' said Mr. Budd, yawning, as the three of them walked back to Larry's house, 'I suppose I'd better be pushin' off. I've got a lot to do tomorrow, and it doesn't look as though I'll reach my bed till late.'

'Why not stop here the night?' suggested Larry, but Mr. Budd refused this invitation.

'I'd rather sleep in my own bed,' he said, 'and I've got to be up fairly early in the mornin'.'

They accompanied him to where he had left his little car, watched him get laboriously in, and waved as he drove off.

The superintendent had not been surprised at the identity of the wild man. He had expected something of the sort, and was glad that the matter had been cleared up. More important things lay before him, and one of these occupied most of his attention throughout the journey back to his little villa at Streatham.

It was nearly twelve o'clock when he reached the quiet street in which he lived, and bringing his car to a halt outside the neat house, got heavily out and opened the double gates that gave admittance to the small garage at the side. Taking a key from his pocket, he unlocked the doors and, pushing them open, came back to his car. He manoeuvred the little machine through the gates and up the concrete path, driving it slowly into the garage. He heard the tinkle of breaking glass as he brought the car to a halt, and smelt the sudden odour of bitter almonds that was wafted to his nostrils.

In a second he had jerked the handkerchief out of his breast pocket, clapped it over his mouth and nostrils, and with surprising agility jumped out of the car. A moment later he was outside the garage in the fresh air of the summer night. And it was a long time before he reentered the little shed.

He let himself into his little house and thoughtfully ate the cold supper his housekeeper had left for him, before he came out again and cautiously put his head inside the garage door. The almond smell was still faintly noticeable, but its pungency had evaporated. Releasing the brakes, the stout man pushed the car out on to the concrete front and then, switching on its headlights so that they illuminated the interior of the garage brightly, went in to investigate.

The remains of a large glass flask were strewn across the floor. This had apparently been attached to a thread that had been stretched across the garage from wall to wall, so that the incoming car had broken it, smashing the flask as it came in contact with the stone floor.

There was no need to wonder what that flask had contained. The almond smell told him that. Hydrocyanic acid, in a concentrated form — one good whiff of which would have meant instant death.

Mr. Budd rubbed the side of his nose and nodded as he stared at the murder contrivance. 'Just the sort of thing he *would* think of,' he muttered, and began to set about locking up the garage preparatory to seeking his bed.

23

Mr. Kyne Prepares His Coup

Mr. Oswald Kyne had been not a little shaken by the unexpected visit from Mr. Budd. It was the first time he had ever come in contact with the police, and he had no wish that it should become a common occurrence.

His unease soon evaporated, however; for if there was one thing Mr. Kyne believed in more than anything else, it was his own ability and astuteness. He was firmly convinced that he was more than a match for the entire police force, and he dismissed any qualms that may have troubled him as a result of the superintendent's visit with this comfortable relief. There was nothing at all to connect him with the dead Sellick, and, so far as his other business dealings were concerned, he had no fear. The people he dealt with were carefully chosen and his tracks equally carefully covered. Even if one of them squealed, it would be very difficult for the law to prove anything against him personally, and without such proof Mr. Kyne was in a position to snap his fingers.

He dressed carefully when Mr. Budd had taken his departure, and coming back to his study, sat down to deal with the matter that was uppermost in his mind.

Time was a consideration. The sooner he got in touch with the man from whom he expected to extract a small fortune, the better. But it was necessary that certain precautions should be attended to first. Mr. Kyne was very interested in his own personal safety, and intended to assure himself that no harm could come to him personally.

Opening a drawer in his desk, he took out several sheets of paper, and for the next hour was busy carefully concocting a document that should safeguard him in any emergency. When he had finished he read it through, made one or two slight alterations, and folding the sheets, enclosed them in an envelope on which he wrote: 'To be opened immediately after my death.'

This envelope he put in a larger one, swiftly scribbled a covering letter, and addressed the bulky packet to his solicitors. Stamping it, he rang for the acid-faced maid and gave it to her with instructions that it was to be posted immediately. When she had withdrawn, he lit a cigar and lay back in his chair with a sigh of relief.

The first part of his preparations was complete. The second part was more difficult, for it relied to a certain extent, on luck, a commodity which Mr. Kyne regarded with an element of suspicion. But although he had racked his brains to try to seek some other way that was more certain, he had completely failed.

Once more he sought paper and pen. Many sheets he discarded before he achieved what he wanted. His final effort read as follows: 'G.J. I know secret, too. Phone. O.K.'

His intention was to have this inserted in the 'personal' column of all the morning papers. If the Grim Joker saw it, he would guess what it meant, but it was very doubtful if anyone else would. There was a possibility that the man it was intended for wouldn't see it at all, and this constituted the element of luck which Mr. Kyne disliked.

His hand was stretched towards the button summoning his servant when the telephone bell rang. He picked up the receiver.

'Is that Mr. Oswald Kyne?' said a man's voice, and when the smooth man had replied in the affirmative: 'I want to see you. I'm afraid I had to treat your associate rather badly, but that was because he was unreasonable.'

'Who are you?' asked Mr. Kyne, though he knew very well to whom he was speaking.

'I think you can guess that. I wrote to you arranging the appointment with your, er, partner.'

Mr. Kyne, who still held the draft of the advertisement, slowly crumpled the paper up in his hand and dropped it into the basket beside his desk. The luck element he had been so chary of had

swung round in his favour. The advertisement was no longer necessary. The man
he wished to reach had forestalled him.

'I'm glad you've rung up,' he said
smoothly, and anyone listening might
have thought that the conversation that
ensued was a very ordinary one carried
on between two businessmen. 'I was
hoping to get in touch with you.'

'I guessed that,' said the Grim Joker. 'I
think we'd better arrange a meeting.'

'Nothing will please me better,'
declared Mr. Kyne, 'provided you're
prepared to discuss business?'

'I haven't any choice,' said the other. 'I
should like you to meet me tomorrow
night at twelve o'clock, at a place I'll
name if you agree.'

'I agree,' said the smooth man. 'But in
case you should be under any misappre-
hension concerning what may occur at
our meeting, I think I'd better tell you
that I've already noted down the, er, gist
of the matter and posted it to my lawyers,
Atkins and Collett, enclosed in an
envelope, stating that it is to be opened
immediately after my death. It will reach

them by the first post in the morning. One has to take these precautions,' he added, almost apologetically.

There was a pause before the other replied. 'You're a clever man,' he said. 'But I've no doubt we can arrange terms. Now listen carefully! Come to Marlow. There's an old houseboat moored to the river bank . . . '

He gave minute directions which Mr. Kyne noted down. 'I'll be there — at twelve o'clock,' he said.

The other rang off, and the money-lender hung up the receiver with a complacent smile. He had been saved a lot of trouble, and if he had thought for a moment, he might have guessed that the Grim Joker would ring him up. He knew that Mr. Kyne shared Sellick's secret and was therefore a danger. No doubt he had intended to eliminate that danger as he had eliminated Sellick. But Mr. Kyne's foresight had rendered any such intention futile. With that letter in the hands of his lawyers, it was in the Grim Joker's interest to keep him alive.

The smooth man chuckled softly. It

was necessary to get up very early in the morning to get the better of Oswald Kyne. Many people had tried it before and failed.

He smoked a cigar thoughtfully, telephoned to his garage for his car, and a few minutes later was sitting at his favourite table in a secluded restaurant discussing with the head waiter a special little dinner that was to celebrate the riches which in his imagination he already saw pouring into his coffers.

24

The Man in the Car.

Larry kept his promise to Norma Grayson early on the following day.

During his walk back with her the night before, he had arranged to pick her up shortly after half-past nine, and he found her ready and waiting when he called at the Larches. They reached Harley Street at eleven. Larry had already phoned Sir John Lannigan making an appointment, and they were shown immediately into the specialist's consulting-room. The kindly-faced grey-haired man greeted Larry with a smile.

'It's a long time since I've seen you, Larry,' he said, shaking hands. 'Don't tell me you've developed the modern complaint of nerves?'

'No, I want to see you about a friend of mine,' Larry answered; and after introducing Norma, he briefly explained the reason for his visit.

Sir John listened interestedly and put several questions to Norma. 'I'll come down and examine your brother tomorrow afternoon,' he said when he had consulted his engagement book. 'At half-past three.'

Larry had some business to attend to in London, and Norma had planned to call on a friend and spend the afternoon shopping. He dropped her at Oxford Circus and set off to keep his two appointments.

He had finished his business by half-past three and was contemplating returning home when it occurred to him that he might drop in and see Mr. Budd. He found that individual in conference with the lugubrious Sergeant Leek.

'Sit down, Larry,' said the superintendent. 'I'll talk to you in a moment. I think this feller's the one we want,' he went on, continuing his conversation with the sergeant. 'He answers the description of the man I was searchin' for. You say he hasn't been seen for a week?'

Leek nodded. 'That's what they say at

his lodgin's,' he answered.

Mr. Budd consulted a report that lay on the desk in front of him. 'Been inside three times for robbery with violence,' he murmured. 'Yes, I'm pretty sure this is the fellow.'

'Who is this desperate criminal?' asked Larry.

The stout man cocked a thoughtful eye at him. 'He's the missin' link in the chain of evidence against the Grim Joker,' he said slowly. 'He's the mistake that all these criminals make.'

'How does he come into it?' demanded his friend.

'He scarcely comes into it at all,' said Mr. Budd, 'but he's very important for all that. Without Bert Liddy, my theory'd fall to the ground.'

'I'd like to know what your theory is,' grunted Larry.

The superintendent smiled. 'It won't be so very long now before everyone knows it,' he said. 'What's brought you up to town?'

Larry told him, and Mr. Budd nodded. 'It was silly to try and hide up that feller,' he said. 'I can understand her reasons. Naturally, bein' fond of him, she was afraid that if the authorities discovered his condition they'd want to shut him up. What does this friend of yours say? Does he think he can cure the feller?'

'He thinks there may be a chance,' answered Larry. 'But of course, he can't tell until he's examined him.'

Mr. Budd scratched his chin. 'How's that man of yours, Clipp, feelin' this mornin'?'

'He looked a bit white about the gills,' said Larry. 'Apparently he was out for a walk when he ran into Grayson and recognised him as the man I'd been enquiring about. His idea was to bring him back to the house, but Grayson insisted on first of all taking him to the place where he had been hiding. He was fairly drunk then, and Clipp thought it was best to humour him. He accompanied him to a deserted barn, and it was his undoing, for Grayson insisted on his having a drink, and that's all Clipp remembers.'

'It's surprisin' he even remembers that,'

commented the stout man. 'I've seen a few drunken fellers in my time, but nothin' to come up to them two. By the way, our Jokin' friend tried to crack one of his gags on me last night.' He told Larry of the flask of poison gas that had been so ingeniously left for him in the garage. 'It was clever and characteristic,' said Mr. Budd, shaking his head. 'And it might very easily have come off. I'll bet he's buyin' all the newspapers today in the hope of readin' an account of my death. Lots of people have tried to kill me, but I'm not so easily got rid of.'

Larry took his departure soon after, and when he had gone Mr. Budd issued certain instructions to Sergeant Leek and went along to have a talk with Chief Inspector Larne. He spent nearly an hour in the chief inspector's office, and when he came out there was a complacent smile on his face, for things were going very well indeed.

There was a popular tea-shop near the Whitehall entrance to Scotland Yard which Mr. Budd occasionally honoured with his presence, and to this he made his way, pausing at the corner of the street to buy an evening paper. As he munched quantities of buttered toast, he scanned the news, and one item interested him.

It was headed:

'OUTRAGE AT SOLICITOR'S OFFICE.'

'What appears to be a senseless practical joke was carried out early this morning at the office of Messrs. Atkins & Collett, solicitors, of Lincoln's Inn Fields. The head clerk, on unlocking the letter-box to get the morning mail, found nothing but a glutinous mass of blackened paper. Someone had apparently poured a quantity of strong sulphuric acid through the letter-box slit, and so destroyed the entire post.

'The police are investigating the matter.'

★   ★   ★

Mr. Budd grunted and turned to the rest of the news. The item was interesting, but it had nothing to do with him.

It was unfortunate that Mr. Oswald Kyne did not see that news item. If he had, it is doubtful he would have looked forward to his meeting with the Grim Joker with so much confidence. For Atkins and Collett were his own lawyers, and among the letters that had been destroyed was the one which he had taken so much pain to concoct, and on which he was relying as protection against any violence that might be offered him at the forthcoming interview.

★　★　★

Norma Grayson spent a pleasant day. She felt as though a great weight had been lifted from her mind, and for the first time for many weeks was free of the worry that had been her constant companion. Her brother's condition had always been a great responsibility, and now that this was to a certain extent shared with Larry Weston, and there was a prospect of his being cured altogether, she felt so light-hearted she could have sung from sheer joy.

She lunched with her friend, who was a cashier in one of the big stores, and afterwards spent a happy afternoon looking at the shops and making one or two purchases she needed. She had tea at the Marble Arch, and coming out of the tea-shop was attracted by the posters outside a cinema. It was a long time since she had been to a film, and she decided that here was a good way of filling in the evening. Her time was her own, and there was nothing to attract her back to the house at Dorking.

She sat through the entire programme and enjoyed it, and it was nine o'clock when she once more found herself in the street. The evening was warm and fine, and after the stuffiness of the picture theatre she elected to walk to the station from which she would get her train home.

She strolled the length of Oxford Street and, reaching Charing Cross Road, decided to take a short cut through to the Strand. It was a narrow street, at this hour quite deserted except for a large saloon car drawn up by the side of the kerb about halfway down. Norma saw this but took no notice of it, and was passing it quickly when a spark of light from the interior attracted her attention and she turned her head.

A man seated in the driving seat was in the act of lighting a cigar, and as the yellow flame of the match illumined his face she stopped dead and stared. The light from a nearby standard fell full on her, and he recognised her at the same instant.

With a muttered exclamation he jerked open the door and sprang out. Two strides and he was by her side, gripping her arm. 'Don't make a sound,' he whispered. 'Come into the car — I want to talk to you.'

Almost before she realised what he was doing, the dazed woman found herself pushed into the dark interior of the saloon. 'I don't understand,' she began huskily. 'What are you — '

The sentence faded to a choking murmur as a heavy hand was clapped over her mouth and nostrils. In a panic of fear, she struggled desperately to free herself from that strangling grasp, but the man's strength was abnormal.

She felt herself forced back on to the cushions of the seat, and his other hand found her throat. She tried to breathe; to shout for help. But the grip tightened, and presently with a last convulsive movement her senses left her and she lay still . . .

25

The Houseboat

The Grim Joker let Norma's limp body fall back onto the padded seat and, pulling a handkerchief from his pocket, wiped his streaming face with a hand that shook.

He had received a severe shock, and it took him a moment or two to recover. It was sheer bad luck that she should have passed down that street just at the moment when he had pulled up to light his cigar — one of those strange coincidences that are more common in fact than in fiction. However, there was no time to think about that, as every second that he remained where he was fraught with danger.

Stooping over Norma, he bound the handkerchief about her mouth, and ripping the lining from her light coat tore it into strips and tied her wrists and ankles. Lifting her from the seat, he arranged her carefully on the floor of the car and covered her with a rug. It was next to impossible now for anyone glancing casually through the window to guess what the car contained.

Stepping out and shutting the door, he got in the front behind the wheel. The engine was still running, and pressing on the clutch pedal he moved the gear lever out of neutral. The big car glided forward, and as he came out of the side street into the Strand he breathed a sigh of relief. The last few minutes had been nasty ones. He felt almost limp from the strain, as though the greater part of his energy had been suddenly drained away.

It was surprising how many unforeseen incidents had occurred, since he had started on his grim purpose, to almost wreck his plans. Sellick and his unpleasant friend, and that fat policeman. Between them they had already forced him to postpone his killing of Austin Barllard. Well, Sellick had been dealt with, and Kyne was due to receive a surprise when he kept the appointment that had been arranged. A smile curved the lips of the car driver as he thought what a surprise it would be. It had been clever of Kyne to send that letter to his lawyers, but the man he was dealing with was cleverer. Nothing had been easier than the pouring of that acid through the letter-slit — the work of less than a minute; and it had rendered Mr. Kyne's careful precautions completely ineffectual.

He chuckled softly. Yes, the blackmailer would undoubtedly get a shock when he turned up at twelve. A shock from which he would never recover, for by that time he would be dead.

The car ran smoothly on through the night. The outskirts of London were soon left behind, and once clear of the traffic he was able to increase his speed, although he was careful to keep within the thirty-mile limit. It would be fatal to be pulled up by a prowling police car with the burden he carried.

He came on to the Bath Road, passed through Slough, and presently, leaving Maidenhead behind, swung to the right and on up the hill leading to Quarry Wood and Marlow. He could catch occasional glimpses of the sheen of the river here, for the road ran close by its bank; and at length, at the edge of a meadow, he brought the car to a stop.

Getting out, he opened a gate and propped it back with a stone. Pausing for a moment, he listened, but there was no sound except the lapping of the water; and returning to the car, he drove it into the field and under the shelter of a thick hedge. When he had switched out the lights it was practically invisible. Opening the door at the back, he lifted Norma out, and from the stiffness of her body guessed that she had recovered consciousness.

Carrying her with difficulty, he stumbled across the uneven surface of the field to a gap in the hedge at the far corner. It was a dark night and he was glad of this, for it reduced the possibility of his being seen. Not that it was a very likely contingency, for it was a lonely spot and nobody came there at this hour.

At the other side of the hedge was a coppice, and beyond this the curve of the river. A dark bulk loomed up under the dropping willows, and near it the Grim Joker paused and laid down his burden. Norma was heavy and he was breathless.

A plank formed a bridge from the bank to the anchored houseboat, and when he had recovered his breath he stooped, picked Norma up once more, and carried her across this precarious way and dropped her on the deck of the boat.

Producing a dark-coloured handkerchief from one of his pockets, he tied it round his head so that it concealed his nose and chin; and finding a key, he unlocked a door giving admittance to the interior of the houseboat.

Austin Barllard, staring up into the darkness, heard him come in and waited for the inevitable scratch of the match that usually accompanied his arrival. It came, the little flame making a splash of yellow in the darkness.

The masked man crossed to the table and lit the lamp, but tonight there was no packet of sandwiches, and the millionaire's heart sank. Did this mean that the end was at hand? For some unknown reason it had been delayed, and his mysterious captor had not carried out his threat. Was tonight to see its fulfilment?

He watched as the other went over to a long, shallow locker and, lifting the lid, brought forth a couple of blankets which he spread on the floor against one wall. When he had done this, he went out again, disappearing into the darkness outside.

Barllard was puzzled. What were the blankets for?

He was soon to be enlightened, for the masked man returned almost immediately, staggering under the weight of the figure he carried.

To his surprise, the millionaire saw that it was a woman. He caught a glimpse of her wide eyes dilated with fear, and wondered. Who was this fresh arrival, and why had she been brought to this place? Was the man a lunatic whose mania took the form of wholesale kidnapping? That certainly seemed the only explanation for his own presence. Ever since he had been brought to this place he had wondered why, and had tried in the long hours to discover a reason, but without result. So far as he could see, there *was* no reason.

The man laid the woman down on the blankets and, straightening up, stood as though in thought. Norma's eyes, roving round the tiny interior of the houseboat, met Barllard's, and he saw the fear in them change to surprise. She was evidently as unprepared to see him as he had been to see her.

The masked man pushed back the cuff of his coat and consulted a watch on his wrist. Without a word he went out once more, this time closing the door behind him.

Norma lay uncomfortably on the rug and stared at the man on the pallet bed opposite her. She had not expected to see him, neither had she the least idea who he was. Someone who was necessary, she supposed, to the successful carrying-out of the horrible plot which accident had revealed to her. Regarding her own fate, she had no illusions. She knew that the man who held her dare not let her go back to the world. For his own safety, she must be silenced. But why had he delayed the inevitable? Why hadn't he killed her at once? Why had he brought her to this place? Was it his intention to keep her a prisoner here until such time as he should choose to kill her?

She shivered. She could force herself to face death calmly, little as she wished to die; but the waiting and suspense were sheer agony. If only he would get it over and done with, while she still possessed a remnant of courage — before her nerves had cracked under the strain.

She thought of Larry and his kindness, and the thought brought tears to her eyes, for it was very unlikely that she would ever see him again. She had no hope of being rescued. When it was discovered that she had not returned to the Larches, her absence would be notified to the police, of course, but it was unlikely that they would ever find her. Certainly not until it was too late. There was nothing to show them where she had been taken. So far as that went she didn't know herself, except that the houseboat was situated on a lonely part of the river.

The outlook seemed quite hopeless;

and with the knowledge of impending death hanging over her, life had never seemed sweeter or more desirable. She closed her eyes, recalling many incidents — stupid, long-forgotten little happenings and experiences that in normal circumstances would never have crossed her mind, but that now filled her brain and took on a significance utterly beyond their worth. She had a sudden longing for one more glimpse of the sun and the sky, for the smell of fresh air after a fall of rain, and for the sight of green leaves, and the shops and the crowded streets. For all the numberless trivial sights and sounds that go to make up that complex fabric of life.

It was wonderful what countless pleasures there were to be had out of the ordinary daily routine of just living — pleasures that she had scarcely noticed or considered until now, when there seemed a prospect of losing them forever. She wondered why everyone who had health and was free could not be happy, and remembered the numerous times she herself had been depressed and miserable for no very particular reason at all. How stupid it all seemed now.

The tears welled up to her eyes, overflowed, and ran slowly down her cheeks until she could taste the salt of them. She might never see the morning come!

She opened her eyes, and through the mist of her tears saw that the man opposite her was watching her gravely. His eyes crinkled as though he was smiling, and he nodded his head.

Once more she wondered who he was and what he was doing here, and how he fitted into the Grim Joker's scheme of things. She wished that her mouth was free of the gag so that she could ask him who he was.

It seemed absurd that such a short while ago she had been sitting in a crowded picture theatre in the heart of London. It almost seemed that her meeting with the man in the car was a dream, a horrible nightmare from which she would shortly wake to find herself back at the Larches in her pretty little bedroom.

There was a movement outside and the

boat rocked, and then the man in the mask came in. He shut the door and, coming to the centre of the little cabin, stood by the table, looking from one to the other. Norma watched him fearfully. She knew only too well what this man was capable of; and presently, when he spoke, her fears were confirmed.

'At half-past twelve tonight,' he said unemotionally, 'my plans will be complete. Owing to circumstances which I could not foresee, I have had to delay my original scheme.' He paused and looked from one to the other. 'In an hour from now you will both cease to live.'

The gag stifled the cry that rose in Norma's throat. She had expected nothing else, but the death sentence when it came destroyed what small amount of hope remained.

26

The Trailer

Mr. Oswald Kyne spent a restless evening. He dined at his usual restaurant, but his nerves were so taut that for the first time in his life he paid little attention to the food that was set before him.

At nine o'clock he came back to his flat, lit a cigar and began pacing up and down his study, speculating on the forthcoming interview. So far as he could see there was no loophole that would give the other an advantage over him.

The newspaper, which he usually read diligently, lay unopened on his desk, for tonight he was too excited to bother about what the rest of the world was doing — and this was his greatest mistake; for had he followed his invariable practice and read that paper, he would have seen the paragraph which, for him, would have meant the difference between life and death. As it was, he was ignorant of the fact that the letter he had so carefully prepared had never reached the hands of the person for whom it was intended; and, being ignorant, was blissfully complacent regarding the result of his meeting with the man he intended to blackmail.

Crossing to a small bookcase, he searched for and found a motoring map of London and its outlying districts. Bringing it back to his desk, he sat down, and with a pencil traced the route he would take and roughly located the position of the houseboat in which he was to meet the Grim Joker. The other's instructions on the telephone had been explicit, and he had very little difficulty in finding the spot. He marked this with a circle, and closing the map laid it in readiness at his elbow.

He had, after long consideration, made one alteration to his plans. It had been his first intention to go alone. On second thought, however, he had decided against this, and the principal reason for his decision had been the fact that he was a little nervous in handling his car. To take his chauffeur was out of the question. The man knew nothing of his employer's methods of earning a living, and would have been shocked had he thought for a moment that his employer was anything but the honest business gentleman he supposed him to be. Mr. Kyne had spent a long time going over in his mind all the various people he knew before he had selected the one most suitable for his purpose.

That afternoon he had telegraphed for Slade, asking that enterprising hotel thief to call and see him at half-past ten. Slade was the very man for the job. He could drive a car and was reliable. Not that Mr. Kyne had the slightest intention of telling him the truth about the business. He had concocted a neat little story about going down to meet a man who had some jewellery to sell, the result of a country house robbery. Slade, he knew, would swallow this without question, and be only too pleased to drive him within walking distance of the meeting place for a hundred pounds or so.

Mr. Kyne poured himself out a stiff drink, gulped half of it and settled down to wait as patiently as he could for the arrival of his associate. Never had the time seemed to go so slowly. Presently, however, he heard the peculiar knock that told him that Slade was outside, and forestalling the thin-lipped housemaid he went out into the hall and opened the door himself.

'What did you send for me for?' asked the man as he came in. 'Has your conscience been pricking you over those emeralds?'

Mr. Kyne conducted him into the study and closed the door. 'There's no reason why it should,' he said, shaking his head. 'I shan't make much profit on them, Slade, I give you my word on that. As I told you, they'll have to be cut up; and by the time I've given my agents a rake-off, there'll be precious little left.'

The hotel thief grunted sceptically. 'Well, what's the idea then?' he demanded.

'Have a drink first and I'll tell you,' said the smooth man.

Slade went over to the sideboard and helped himself to a whisky and soda.

'Now,' said Mr. Kyne, seating himself behind his desk, 'pull up your chair and listen to me.'

The other did so and he began to tell his story. It must be said in justice to him that he told it very well. No one hearing it, and knowing Mr. Kyne's little peculiarities, would have doubted it for a moment. Slade, as he expected, never even questioned the truth of his statement.

'And you want me to drive you down to this place and drive you back?' he asked.

Mr. Kyne nodded. 'That's it exactly. I want you to put me down within a hundred yards of this houseboat and wait until I come back. I shan't be more than half an hour at the outside. There's a hundred of the best for your trouble.'

'In advance?' asked Slade suspiciously.

Mr. Kyne made a gesture of annoyance. 'If you like,' he answered. 'You don't think I'd double-cross you, do you, Slade?'

'You would if you got half the chance. I'll drive better if I've got that hundred in my pocket.'

Mr. Kyne put his hand in his breast pocket and took out a fat wallet. From this he extracted the hundred in ten-pound notes, and threw them across the desk. 'There you are,' he said. 'The labourer is worthy of his hire.'

Slade counted them carefully and stowed them away in an inner pocket. He was not quite sure if the 'labourer' part of it was a compliment, but a hundred pounds was not always picked up so easily, and he could afford to dispense with petty politenesses.

Mr. Kyne produced his motoring map and pointed out the route he had marked. Slade glanced at it and nodded. 'I know my way about pretty well,' he said. 'You needn't bother with that. There's very few places I don't know the quickest way of getting to.'

He helped himself to one of Mr. Kyne's cigars and they sat talking, mostly about a job the hotel thief had planned for the future, the proceeds of which would eventually find their way into Mr. Kyne's possession.

The hands of the clock were pointing to eleven when the smooth man decided that it was time to make a move. They left the flat and walked quickly towards the garage; and a car that had been waiting, drawn up near the kerb, followed slowly in their wake. It waited near the entrance as they went in, and presently, when Mr. Kyne's car emerged, the other machine followed it, keeping at a discreet distance, and never losing sight of it for a single instant. At the field where earlier that evening the Grim Joker had stopped his own car, Mr. Kyne signalled to Slade to pull up.

'This is the place,' he muttered. 'The houseboat lies a few hundred yards upstream.' He got out of the car heavily and gave his final instructions to the man at the wheel. 'Wait here until I come back — and you'd better put your lights out. We don't want to advertise our presence if there should happen to be anyone wandering about.' Slade nodded and the powerful lights dimmed.

Mr. Kyne made his way across the oblong of meadowland. He had some difficulty in finding the gap in the hedge, but eventually succeeded, and negotiating the miniature wood found himself on the riverbank. He had gone a considerable distance and was beginning to wonder if he had made a mistake when he saw a shadowy bulk loom out of the darkness, and drawing nearer discovered that it was the houseboat he was seeking.

He felt no fear as he approached, no misgivings that any harm could come to him. The letter, which he imagined reposed safely in the possession of his solicitors, safeguarded him from all possibility of sharing the fate that had overtaken the unfortunate Sellick. His forthcoming interview would be easy. It was almost like taking money from a child's money-box.

He was confident and optimistic as he crossed the plank leading from the bank to the little deck of the houseboat and tapped at the door. There came to his ears the sound of a shuffling movement from inside, and then the lock clicked and the door was opened an inch.

'Is that Kyne?' asked a voice softly, and the smooth man saw a figure partly obliterating the dim crack of light.

'It is,' he answered, and the door was opened wider.

'Come in,' said the Grim Joker, and when Mr. Kyne had crossed the threshold, shut and relocked the door. 'Now, let's complete this business as quickly as possible, for at dawn I am leaving England for good.'

27

An Urgent Call

When Larry Weston left Scotland Yard, he had every intention of returning immediately to Dorking. He had barely, however, negotiated the wide archway and brought his little car into the broad thoroughfare of Whitehall when a voice hailed him from the pavement, and looking round he saw an old friend of his waving frantically for him to stop. He brought his car to a halt at the sidewalk and the other joined him.

Teddy Loring was a cheery red-faced man in his mid-fifties. He had been in the same regiment as Larry during the war, had received his commission at the same time, and shared a dugout in the front line. It was some time since they had met, and Larry was genuinely pleased to see his friend. Loring suggested that they should go along to tea at his club, and since there was no pressing need for Larry to get back to Dorking he accepted. The other squeezed into the seat beside him, and they set off in the direction of Piccadilly.

Over tea in the spacious smoking-room, they discussed various things that had happened to them since their last meeting, and it was six o'clock when Larry ventured to suggest that he ought to be going.

'What's the hurry, old boy?' said Teddy Loring. 'It isn't often I see you. There's no reason to go scuttling away so soon. Look here, I tell you what — let's have a bit of dinner together. We can either go out or have it here.'

'We'll go out,' answered Larry. 'The dinner's on me.'

Teddy argued about this, but Larry insisted, and with a resigned shrug of his shoulders the elder man capitulated.

They had a glass of the club's best dry sherry and set off in search of a little restaurant near Piccadilly Circus where Larry invariably dined when he was in town. The food was good, and over it they continued their reminiscences. It was half-past nine when Larry walked back with his friend to the club to pick up his little car, which he had left outside that establishment.

'We must fix another meeting for next week,' insisted Loring. 'I've got your telephone number and I'll give you a ring.'

Larry agreed, and shaking hands with his friend got into his car and began to thread his way through the traffic.

For some reason his anxiety to get back had left him. The brilliant lights and the bustle and confusion around him compared, in his present mood, favourably with the quietness of his country home. His main reason for originally wishing to get back early had been the possibility of an hour with Norma Grayson, but by the time he got back it would be too late to call on her.

Quite suddenly he made up his mind. He would go back to Scotland Yard and see if Mr. Budd was still there.

He put this plan into execution and learned from the doorman on duty that the stout superintendent was still in his office. Mr. Budd's large face showed his surprise as he came in.

'What, you here again?' he grunted. 'What's the matter?'

'Nothing's the matter,' said Larry, 'only I've been dining with a friend, ran into him accidentally just after I left you, and I'm feeling restless.'

Mr. Budd sighed wearily, and extracting a cigar from his waistcoat pocket, looked at it gloomily. 'I was just thinkin' of goin' home,' he said, 'but I'm glad you've come all the same. I've got a hunch there may be somethin' in the air tonight.'

'What sort of something?' demanded his friend.

'Just somethin',' replied the other vaguely. 'It's a funny thing, but I have these hunches sometimes. It's a sort of sixth sense that tells me when somethin's goin' to happen.'

'Indigestion!' said Larry promptly.

'Maybe,' answered Mr. Budd, carefully removing the band from his cigar. 'Maybe it's somethin' with a more scientific name. Anyway, it's the cause of my being here at this hour. I've been meanin' to go home ever since seven o'clock, and kept on puttin' it off and puttin' it off because of this feelin'.'

'Or because you're too lazy to move,' said Larry. 'Have you got any fresh news?'

The stout man searched in his pocket for his matches, and lit his cigar before replying. 'No,' he answered slowly, 'if you mean about this Grim Joker business. I think the next news I shall have about that is the arrest of the feller.'

'I wish you'd tell me who you think it is.'

The other shook his head. 'I don't *think*, I *know*, but I'm not tellin' you, Larry. At any moment now I may have the feller himself under lock and key, and until that time arrives I'm not sayin' anythin'.'

'You're an aggravating old devil,' growled his friend. 'I don't believe you've the faintest idea who the man is, but when you've caught him you'll pretend that you knew all along.'

Mr. Budd smiled. 'Maybe that's it,' he

answered blandly. 'Maybe I'm like these detectives you read about who are always makin' cryptic statements with nothin' to back 'em up. And maybe I'm not.' He leaned back in his chair. 'When this business is finished, an' you learn the ins and outs of it, you'll realise that what I've been sayin' is the truth.'

'If you really know who this fellow is, why don't you arrest him?'

'I said I know *who* he is,' replied the stout man, 'but I didn't say I know *where* he is. That's what I'm waitin' for. And I'm hopin' that a certain gentleman I know, who isn't such a gentleman either, will show me. I could issue a description in the usual way, but I don't want to scare my bird. He's a pretty clever feller, and if he once got an inklin' that I really knew him, he might pop off for good. What I'm hopin' is — '

The telephone bell shrilled and cut into his sentence, and reaching out his hand the superintendent picked up the receiver. 'Speakin',' he said, and listened to the message that came over the wire. 'Just gone in, has he? Well, now, be extra careful and don't lose sight of either of 'em.' He dropped the instrument back on its rest and looked at Larry. 'My hunch looks like comin' off,' he remarked.

'Who was that?' asked the other interestedly.

'That was Detective Constable Flyman. He's a member of the Flyin' Squad. And he and Sergeant Bowman are watchin' the place where this feller I mentioned lives. A man called Slade has just paid him a visit.' He nodded several times. 'Yes, I think things may be movin'.'

'Who's Slade?'

'Slade's a very clever feller, because he's never had a conviction, though it's my own opinion he ought to be doin' seven years. He's a classy hotel thief, but we've never been able to prove anythin' against him.'

Larry frowned perplexedly. 'But what's he got to do with the Grim Joker?'

'So far as I know,' answered Mr. Budd calmly, 'he's got nothin' to do with him. But the feller he's just gone to see may have quite a lot to do with him. It was he who took Sellick to Quarry Wood on the night he was killed. I've got evidence to prove that, and I could pull him in this minute if I wanted to. He told me he hadn't been out that night, but a policeman on point duty saw him bring the car back to his garage and recognised both him and the machine.'

'Well, I suppose you know what you're talking about,' said Larry resignedly, 'but I'm hanged if I do.'

'I never speak unless I know what I'm talkin' about,' said Mr. Budd severely. 'And now I'll tell you somethin'. I'm not goin' to tell you the name of this Jokin' feller, but I'll tell you the reason behind the jokes.'

Larry stared at him incredulously. 'You know?'

'I know everythin',' answered the stout man extravagantly. In his slow, husky voice he began, and Larry listened, his amazement growing as his friend proceeded. When he came to the end of his long narrative, a great light burst on Larry.

'Good Lord!' he exclaimed. 'Then the Grim Joker must be — '

'Don't say it, Larry,' interrupted Mr. Budd, 'but I think you're right.'

Larry sat staring at him in stunned silence, and before he could speak again the telephone bell rang.

'Hello!' said Mr. Budd, and after listening for a few seconds he became galvanised into action. With his free hand he pressed a button on his desk. 'All right, I'll attend to that,' he said. 'Relay any further messages at once.'

As he hung up the receiver, the door opened and a messenger came in.

'Order a fast car to be ready in two minutes,' snapped the superintendent, 'and find Sergeant Leek and send him to me at once.'

The messenger withdrew, and he glanced at the clock. Following his glance, Larry saw with surprise that it was nearly midnight. 'Good Lord!' he exclaimed. 'I'd no idea I'd been here so long. I must be — '

'You'd better stay and see the end of this business now,' grunted the stout man.

'The end?'

'Yes. That telephone message was from

Imber Court, where they've transferred the wireless room that used to be in Scotland House. They've just received a wireless message from Squad Car WA17. Sergeant Bowman has trailed that feller Kyne from his flat to Marlow — '

He broke off as the door opened and Sergeant Leek came in. To him he issued a string of instructions. 'And pick up three automatics from the armoury department,' he ended.

The sergeant blinked rapidly and withdrew.

'Come on,' said Mr. Budd. 'Our car ought to be ready.' Moving faster than Larry had ever seen him move, he left his office and hurried down the stairs to the vestibule. As Larry joined him on the broad steps, a police tender drew up in front of them.

Mr. Budd bundled his friend into the back and got in beside him. 'As soon as Leek joins us we'll be off,' he muttered.

The sergeant appeared a minute later. 'Here you are,' he said, and handed Mr. Budd two ugly-looking automatics. 'They're both loaded.'

'All right,' said the stout man. 'Get in the front with the driver. Tell him to go as fast as he can to Marlow.'

The long-faced sergeant obeyed, and as the car moved off the superintendent handed one of the automatics to Larry. 'You'd better take this,' he grunted. 'You may need it.'

Larry felt a tingling of excitement as they came out of the Embankment entrance and swung over Westminster Bridge. Would the end of their journey see also the end of the Grim Joker?

He was thankful that caprice had prompted him to return to Scotland Yard that night. But for that he would not have been in at the death. The phrase sounded melodramatic, and he smiled; but he little knew how apt it was, nor that this headlong rush through the darkness was destined to save the life of the woman who meant more to him than anything else in the world.

28

The Motive

Mr. Oswald Kyne looked curiously round the dimly lighted interior of the houseboat. His eyes stared with wonder as he caught sight of the manacled figure of the millionaire lying on the pallet bed; passed from him to the helpless woman on the blankets with deepening amazement.

'Who are these people?' he asked, and seeing the surprise on his face the man in the mask chuckled.

'The gentleman is Mr. Austin Barllard,' he replied in his thin, squeaky voice. 'A most important person. The — '

'The — the millionaire?' gasped Mr. Kyne, for he had read of the disappearance of the tobacco magnate, and, like the rest of the world, had wondered. 'What's he doing here?'

'He's here for a purpose,' answered the Grim Joker, 'and that purpose reaches its maturity tonight.' He chuckled. 'It's lucky that Mr. Barllard is an orphan and has no encumbrances such as a wife or children, for after you've gone he's going on a long journey, and it would be a pity if there was anyone who would miss him.'

His meaning was unmistakable, and the smooth man shivered. 'You mean you're going to kill him?' he whispered huskily.

'That's my intention,' said the other calmly. 'That's the reason why I've been keeping him here for so long.'

'And the woman?' asked Mr. Kyne, who had never seen Norma Grayson before and therefore failed to recognise her.

'She is a lady,' replied the Grim Joker, 'who's accidentally been the means of nearly spoiling my plans. I'm afraid, therefore, that she'll have to share the fate of Mr. Barllard.'

'But — why have you waited?' enquired the astonished Mr. Kyne. 'If you wanted to kill Barllard, why didn't you do so before? You've run an enormous risk keeping — '

'I know, but the time wasn't ripe,'

interrupted the other impatiently. 'Tomorrow the papers will come out with the news that the body of Mr. Austin Barllard has been found on the Bath Road — er — stabbed to the heart. There will be a lot of speculation as to how he got there and the reason for his death. But I doubt very much if anyone will hit on the true solution of the mystery.' He paused and turned his head in the direction of the millionaire. 'I don't think even Mr. Barllard himself knows that,' he continued, 'but since he will shortly be in the only condition in which a human being can be trusted with a secret, we might, I think, satisfy his curiosity.'

Again he paused and chuckled. Norma, whose heart had momentarily beat faster with hope when she had heard the arrival of Mr. Kyne, stared at him with eyes that were pools of fear.

'Fifteen years ago, Mr. Barllard,' continued the Grim Joker, addressing the helpless man, 'you were rescued from a fire at the Metro-Palace Hotel, Brighton, by a Mr. Hamilton Lorne and Mr. Percival Haynes. At great personal risk to themselves, they got you out of the burning building just before it collapsed. During the process, however, you were so badly burned and suffered such a severe shock that, although you were rushed to the nearest hospital, your life was despaired of. For days you lay in a critical condition; but owing to the skill of Dr. Roone and the untiring attention of Miss Julia Rothe, the nurse who looked after you, you were slowly dragged from the shadow of death. You never expected to see the world again; and during your convalescence, in gratitude to the people who saved your life, you made a will.'

The steady eyes of the millionaire lit up with a flash of understanding, and the masked man nodded as he saw it. 'I see that you've guessed the rest,' he said. 'You had no living kith or kin, and you left your entire fortune to be equally divided between the four people whose efforts were the direct cause of your being alive. And you further stipulated that should any of them die before your own decease, the remaining ones should benefit pro-rata, so that if only one remained alive at the time of your death, he or she would receive the entire amount of which you died possessed. It was a generous scheme. I made enquiries, and I found that the sum involved is just over a million and a quarter pounds.'

Mr. Kyne gasped, and his eyes glittered avariciously as the other finished. 'And this — this comes to you?' he whispered.

'It comes to me indirectly,' assented the Grim Joker, 'after . . . ' He paused significantly. ' . . . the death of Mr. Austin Barllard has been proved.'

The smooth man's mind was working busily. He had had no idea that such a vast sum was at stake, and mentally he cursed himself for having put his own demands so low. However, he brightened as the thought entered his head that it could be treated, after all, as a first instalment. There would be larger pickings later. He felt no horror at the other's calmly announced intention of adding two additional murders to his other crimes. Greed and the thought of the enormous sum involved had swamped all other emotions.

The Grim Joker seemed to read his thoughts to a certain extent, for he said after a brief pause: 'You want fifty thousand pounds, don't you, as the price of your silence?'

Mr. Kyne looked at him. 'Two hundred thousand,' he murmured gently.

'Sellick said fifty thousand,' said the man in the mask sharply.

The smooth man smiled apologetically. 'I'm not responsible for what Sellick said. He was a common little crook, and fifty thousand to him must have appeared a fortune. Besides, he was unaware of the amount involved. I'm sure, had he known, that he would've raised his price.'

The other uttered an oath.

'After all,' went on Mr. Kyne, 'what's two hundred thousand out of a million and a quarter? A mere nothing. Be reasonable, my dear sir — you are not paying me for nothing. My silence is essential to your safety. If I open my lips, you'll not only get none of the money you've schemed for, but you'll be hanged into the bargain. Surely you won't risk this unpleasantness for the sake of two hundred thousand pounds?'

'Aren't you afraid to threaten me?' muttered the Grim Joker.

Mr. Kyne smiled complacently. 'Why should I be afraid? You dare not harm me. If anything happens to me at this moment, you'd be in a very serious position. You must realise that. The letter I forwarded to my solicitors contains full details of my knowledge. In the event of my death it will be opened immediately, with disastrous results to yourself.'

The other was silent, and thinking he had impressed him, Mr. Kyne went on: 'There's no point in our haggling over terms. If you don't agree, you will be the loser, and I've no doubt that Mr. Barllard would be willing to pay me an equivalent sum to that I am asking you to, er, save his life.'

For a moment the man in the mask was incapable of speech, so great was the rage that mastered him; but with a supreme effort he choked it down. When he spoke, except for a slight tremble in the tone, it was the same squeaky voice as heretofore: 'All right, I'll make it two hundred thousand. But you won't get a penny more, you understand? And you won't get that for several weeks.'

'I don't mind waiting,' answered Mr. Kyne generously. 'I am not, er, exactly in need of money. So long as I get what I want in the end, I don't mind waiting.'

'You'll get that.'

'I'm glad you're being sensible. I shall expect my share the day after you draw your own money. And I warn you that if it doesn't arrive punctually, I shall inform the police immediately concerning your real identity. I think that is all.' He crossed over to the door. 'I'll be getting back to my car. I don't wish to keep my driver waiting longer than I can help.'

'You — you brought somebody with you?' hissed the Grim Joker angrily.

'A man called Slade,' answered Mr. Kyne. 'You need have no fear; he knows nothing about our business.'

The other unlocked the door. 'Where did you leave your car?' he asked casually.

'By the edge of the field,' replied Kyne, stepping through the opening onto the little deck. 'Now don't forget, I shall expect my money the day after yours comes into your possession.'

'You'll get nothing,' snarled the man at his side. 'You fool! D'you think I don't know that the two hundred thousand would only be a first instalment, and that for the rest of my life I should have you draining me like a leech?'

The smooth man shrugged his shoulders. 'Well, I don't see how you can help it.'

'There *is* one way,' said the Grim Joker, speaking in his natural voice. 'You thought you were clever, didn't you, writing that letter to your lawyers — but it never reached them. I'm just a little cleverer than you, Kyne, and I took precautions to see that it was destroyed.'

Mr. Kyne's face went deathly white, and fear gripped his heart. 'You're lying — ' he began, but the sentence was never completed, for the other drove the knife he had slipped from his pocket sharply upwards, and with a choking cry Kyne collapsed onto his knees and fell forward in a heap.

The Grim Joker bent down, made sure he was quite dead, and toppled the body gently into the swiftly running river.

29

The Last Joke

With a cigarette between his lips, Slade slumped back in the driving seat of Mr. Kyne's car and stared into the darkness of the night. The crisp notes that reposed in his pocket, added to the sum he had already got for the emeralds, would keep him in affluence until he had completed the plans for his next job.

He already had his eye on the jewels of a foreign princess who was visiting England. But he was a very careful man, and planned his coups down to the last detail. It was to this care that he attributed his success. He never made the mistake of staying in the same hotel as his prospective victim, but worked from one nearby, and took elaborate precautions to ensure that he had a watertight alibi in case of accidents. He had several good friends who, for a consideration, were willing to commit perjury and swear, should any suspicion attach to him, that he was in their company at the time the robbery was committed. He was thinking over his new plan when, looking up, he saw a shadowy figure approaching. It paused a few yards away and beckoned hurriedly. Concluding that it was Mr. Kyne, he muttered a curse, got out of the car, and walked towards the other.

'What do you want?' he called.

'I want you,' hissed a squeaky voice, and too late Slade realised it was not his employer who had beckoned to him. Before he could rectify his mistake, two strong hands leaped to his throat and buried themselves in his flesh. With the cries strangled in his mouth, Slade bent backwards, struggling desperately to free himself from that choking grip.

Tighter and tighter it grew, until his tongue protruded and his eyes bulged. Flashes of red shot across the blackness that was enveloping him. He felt his senses swimming, and an indescribable languor stealing over him, and then —

'Let go that man and put up your

hands!' snapped a harsh voice, and out of the night sprang a bright beam of light.

The Grim Joker released his hold of the unfortunate hotel thief and looked up as the torch focused on him, and looking, saw the huge bulk of Mr. Budd.

'I want you, my Jokin' friend,' said the stout man quietly, and advanced towards the masked figure, a long-barrelled automatic held unwaveringly in front of him.

He had barely taken three steps, however, when, by one of those freaks of chance that sometimes seem to play into the hands of the evil-doer, his foot caught in a rut and he stumbled.

Quick as a flash, the Grim Joker took advantage of the accident. Jerking the semi-conscious body of Slade up by the collar, he flung him at the superintendent, so that he struck against that stout man's ankles even as Mr. Budd was recovering from his fatal stumble.

The result was disastrous. Losing his balance completely, the detective went sprawling at full length, his pistol flying from his hand as he did so.

The masked man turned swiftly at the same moment and went racing towards Mr. Kyne's deserted car, and hurling himself into the driving seat, thrust frantically at the self-starter.

'Come here, Leek, quickly!' yelled Mr. Budd as he struggled to his feet and tried to run towards the throbbing car, but he had wrenched his ankle in his fall and could do no more than hobble. Even as the thin sergeant loomed out of the darkness, the saloon jerked forward and went tearing down the road.

'Quick!' panted the stout man, pointing to the rapidly vanishing car. 'Get Bowman and follow him. Pick me up as you go by — I can't walk. Hurry, or we'll lose him.' The melancholy sergeant grunted and disappeared into the darkness again at a run.

It seemed an age to Mr. Budd before the blazing headlights of the squad car swept towards him and stopped with a grinding of brakes, but in reality barely fifty seconds elapsed between the time of the Grim Joker's escape and his own start in pursuit.

Larry's strong arm pulled the detective on board. The driver slipped in the clutch and, with scarcely a pause, the powerful car bounded forward and went rushing off in the wake of its quarry.

'There he is,' grunted Mr. Budd, and the driver nodded. The car in front was going like the wind, and even as they looked, vanished into a patch of dense shadow cast by some overhanging trees.

On and on they went, the miles reeling behind them. Suddenly Larry gave a triumphant exclamation. 'We're gaining, Budd,' he cried exultantly. 'Go on, driver, let her rip!'

And he was right, as Mr. Budd saw as he peered ahead. The distance between pursuer and pursued had appreciably lessened. There was a sharp curve in the road in front, and round this the fugitive car skidded almost on two wheels and they lost sight of it. Taking the bend themselves at full speed, the Rosebud gave a warning shout, for the Grim Joker had pulled the saloon up and left it broadside in their path. The road was narrow and the big car blocked it effectually from side to side. The police-driver saw the danger and realised that it was impossible to pull up in time. He applied the brakes and jerked frantically at the wheel.

With screaming brake-drums the huge machine swerved, bumped dizzily over the uneven clumps of turf that bordered the road, and crashed into a straggling hedge. The windscreen shivered to fragments, and the occupants were almost jerked from their seats at the shock of the impact. Fortunately beyond a few bruises no one was hurt, and as they scrambled out the superintendent caught sight of a flying figure against the greenish-blue of the skyline.

'There he is!' he shouted. 'After him, Leek! I'm useless because of my ankle, but you and Bowman can get him.'

The Grim Joker heard his voice and looked back, panting as he stumbled over the rough ground. With a bit of luck he ought to get away — the country here was wild, the ground studded with gorse bushes, and ahead the fringe of a big wood. If he could only reach the shelter of that, there was a chance for him.

He heard the thud of pursuing feet and redoubled his speed, but he was out of condition and the pace was too hot to keep up. There came a sharp stabbing pain in his side and his breath became laboured, whistling through his throat in great gasps. The gorse bushes were growing more thickly now, so that he had to force his way through them, tearing his hands and face on the sharp spines.

Suddenly, to his horror, he saw the reflection of a light strike the leaves in front of him. One of his pursuers had produced an electric torch and was fanning it across the common. Capture seemed inevitable; the muscles of his legs ached and his feet were heavy, as though encased in leaden shoes.

Desperately he clenched his teeth and ran on, doubling from side to side in the hope of outwitting them, but the approaching steps grew steadily nearer. The handkerchief about his nose and mouth impeded his breathing and he tore it away, throwing it from him.

Presently the ground began to slope

sharply, giving an additional speed, and his heart beat hopefully. But it was too late. He heard a shout close behind him; heard the hiss of panting breath, and as an outstretched hand reached forward to grasp his shoulder gave one last leap to escape those clutching fingers.

He landed on something that crumbled beneath his feet, tried vainly to recover his balance and found himself falling —

He struck a sharp object, and the impact made him shriek aloud with pain. His wild hands grasped despairingly at tree and shrub and grass, slipped, and again he was falling . . . down . . . down . . . down . . .

★ ★ ★

The pink of a summer dawn was streaking the sky in the east when they found him lying huddled up at the bottom of a sheer drop that led down to the valley — a twisted, sprawling figure with neck awry, the face stamped with the fear of that last moment.

'A pretty terrible end, but he deserved

it,' said Mr. Budd gravely, looking down at all that remained of the Grim Joker. 'Dr. Roone was a clever man, almost a perfect criminal, but his last joke rebounded against himself.'

Larry nodded. 'You were right,' he said.

'Of course I was right,' grunted the Rosebud. 'I'm the only detective in the force who's never been known to make a mistake!'

Leek's lugubrious voice broke in on this outrageous statement. 'I'll go and phone for an ambulance,' he said.

30

Mr. Budd Has the Final Word

'It was you who were really to blame for the Grim Joker,' said Mr. Budd some hours later, looking across Larry Weston's drawing-room with sleepy eyes to where Mr. Austin Barllard sat at his ease smoking one of Larry's cigars with obvious enjoyment.

'Yes, I'm afraid it was,' admitted the millionaire, 'and it shows you that even gratitude has a nasty habit of stinging at times.' He looked haggard and ill, but the meal he had recently consumed — the first decent one for weeks — had done much to restore him to something like his normal spirit.

After attending to the details made necessary by the tragic death of Dr. Roone, Mr. Budd, Larry, and the sergeant had driven back to the houseboat and released Barllard and Norma Grayson.

She had been almost in a state of collapse, but when she found that all danger was over she quickly recovered, and except for an unusual paleness looked little the worse for her terrifying ordeal.

'I'm still a little puzzled as to the meaning of it all,' she confessed. 'What did Dr. Roone hope to gain by all these crimes?'

'A million and a quarter pounds,' answered the Rosebud. 'Quite a nice little round sum of money. People have killed before for less than half that amount.'

He paused and took a pull at one of his long black cigars.

'It wasn't until he lost his money in a disastrous deal on the stock exchange,' he continued, 'and was rackin' his brains to find some means to replenish his exchequer, that he remembered the fire at Brighton, and the will that Mr. Barllard had caused to be drawn up in gratitude to the people who had rescued him. Thinkin' it over, he remembered the actual terms of the will. He was present, I believe, when it was made.'

He looked across at the millionaire for confirmation and Barllard nodded. 'Quite right, he was,' he said a little grimly.

'There took form in his brain,' Mr. Budd went on, ' — and I'm sure that the worry he was passing through must have affected his sanity a little and caused him to lose sight of values — which later bore fruit in the birth of the Grim Joker. The terms of the will — I've seen a copy at the solicitors', by the way — are to the effect that your entire fortune in the event of your death is to be equally divided between the four people who had been the cause of savin' your life during the fire at the Metro-Palace. They were Lorne, Haynes, Miss Rothe, and Dr. Roone himself. In the event of any of these people dyin' before you, their share was to go to their nearest livin' relative; and if there was no relative livin', to be added to the amount to be distributed among those of the four who remained alive.

'The Grim Joker would never have come into existence at all if Roone hadn't discovered on making enquiries that the people who stood in his way from receivin' the full amount of your fortune were without kith or kin. It was this fact which must have first suggested the plan of campaign, which he afterwards carried out.

'His first proceedin' — and I'm now no longer guessin' but statin' what actually occurred — was to establish the fact that he possessed a brother. He mentioned him to several of his acquaintances, including Miss Grayson. Then he went over to Paris and took a flat in the name of James Roone, in which he installed a housekeeper, givin' out to her that he travelled a lot and would only be there now and again at irregular intervals. The letters he received from his supposed brother he wrote himself, leavin' them with this woman to post at stated intervals. When he used to go on a visit to his supposed brother, he was in reality becomin' that very brother, just returned from one of his trips, and for this purpose he appeared in Paris disguised in a slight beard.

'Havin' prepared a way for the last act

in the drama he contemplated, he proceeded to stage the first and kidnapped Mr. Barllard. Takin' him to the houseboat he'd bought in another name, he kept him a prisoner here, ready to be killed when the moment was ripe. And here he certainly showed undoubted cleverness. He realised that if Lorne, Haynes, and Julia Rothe were murdered in the ordinary way, someone might discover the true motive, so he conceived of the mysterious personality of the Grim Joker, and devised the card and the rhymin' warnin' to make it appear that the crimes were the work of a homicidal maniac.'

'He damn well succeeded, too,' interrupted Larry with a grunt. 'I for one was convinced they were.'

'So were most people,' said Mr. Budd, shaking his head sadly, 'and it just shows you the fallacy of jumpin' to conclusions. Now I never thought these crimes were the work of a lunatic, and I was right.'

He looked round complacently and then continued: 'Allowin' a fairly long lapse of time to take place between each murder so that no one should suspect any possible connection between the victims, Roone succeeded in gettin' rid of the three people who stood in his way, and then put into practice the plan that was to eliminate any chance of suspicion fallin' on himself — as it might have done when the will was read and it was found that he'd inherited Mr. Barllard's fortune. He sent himself one of the Grim Joker's cards and rang me up to tell me that he'd received it. It was almost a stroke of genius.'

'Who — who was it, then, who was killed?' asked Norma in a low voice during the short pause that followed.

'The man the doctor had engaged to put through the false telephone call purporting to come from me,' answered Mr. Budd a little grimly. 'It was the first time he'd used a confederate, and he took care that his accomplice shouldn't have the chance of squealin'. Everythin' was planned very carefully. The man, whose name was Bert Liddy, was dressed as a telephone inspector. The call was put through from a house less than two hundred yards from Roone's own. He called with the plausible excuse of testin' the telephone, contrived to be alone, and phoned the message that took Roone out. Roone left in his car, but instead of goin' towards Dorkin' he ran the car into a little lane in the opposite direction, where he'd already arranged to meet his assistant. And there he killed the man and changed his clothes.

'Unfortunately for him, Sellick, who was a crook, had followed him and witnessed the murder. He threatened to give Roone away unless he paid him to keep silent, and the doctor had to promise to keep in touch with him to save his whole scheme from tumbling to the ground.'

'I'm surprised he didn't murder Sellick as well,' said Barllard.

'I expect he would have done,' replied the stout man, 'but it might have upset his plans. He made up for it later, however, and shot the man in Quarry Wood when he came to get the promised money.'

'Then it was Dr. Roone himself who

telephoned to you about — about the . . . ' Norma hesitated, leaving the sentence unfinished.

Mr. Budd nodded ponderously. 'Yes. He must've waited until he saw us arrive, placed the body in the wheatfield as we found it, adopted some sort of disguise, and leavin' the car by the side of the road walked into Dorkin' and sent that message.'

'Why did he keep Mr. Barllard a prisoner?' asked Larry. 'Why didn't he kill him at once?'

'Because he had no intention of killin' him until all the others, includin' himself, had met their death. If he'd have killed him, the will would have come to light. His plan was to keep Barllard locked up in the houseboat, where he could find him exactly when he wanted to; and when he had completed the rest of his scheme, murder him and leave him somewhere where his body would be found and identified. Roone would then have gone off to Paris, and after a lapse of a week or so, in which time his beard would have grown, he would have turned up in his flat as his brother — '

'To find himself the inheritor of one million and a quarter pounds,' finished Austin Barllard.

'That's right,' agreed Mr. Budd. 'For, by the terms of your will, Dr. Roone's brother, bein' next of kin, would have got the lot.'

'But I don't understand,' said Norma, frowning perplexedly. 'His brother called one day at the Larches. I think I told you.'

'You did,' said Mr. Budd. 'And Dr. Roone was out at the time. It was Roone himself, disguised in his little beard, who called to see — himself!'

'But,' protested Norma, 'they were together in the library.'

'Did you see 'em together?'

She shook her head.

'Of course you didn't. Dr. Roone entered his study as his brother, slipped out of the window, removed his beard, and came back as himself. Naturally he was told his brother was waitin' and went straight into the room he'd just left. I bet you didn't see the brother depart?'

'No, I didn't. Dr. Roone sent me down

to the post office.'

'And I'll bet he sent Sellick on some other errand, too,' remarked the Rosebud, 'and when you both got back this mythical brother of his had gone — back to Paris.'

Norma gave a little shiver. 'I shall never forget the shock I had when I recognised him in the car. I thought I'd seen a ghost.'

'Must've been a pretty big shock for him, too. He must've realised the danger of his whole carefully planned scheme fallin' to pieces. That was the night, Slade tells me, that he'd arranged to meet Kyne. You can thank your stars, young lady, that you're still alive.'

He flicked a cylinder of ash from his cigar into the fireplace, and there was a long silence, broken at last by Larry.

'How did that five-pound note get into the pocket of the dead man?' he asked.

'I can only guess at that,' Mr. Budd replied, 'but I should think the most possible explanation is that while Roone was spyin' out the land before killin' Julia Rothe, he had occasion to buy somethin' at Horsham and received the five-pound note in change. Obviously he didn't notice her name and address on the back, or he wouldn't have left it in his notecase.'

'How did you first become suspicious that Roone was the Grim Joker?' asked Larry.

Mr. Budd smiled. 'It was the dead man's shoes that first put the idea in my head. They were two sizes too large for the feet on which they were placed, and I began to wonder. I thought it all over, and everythin' seemed to point to Roone. And then, when the pathologist examined the body, I got confirmation of my idea. The man hadn't any teeth, it was true, but the false ones in his mouth were never made to fit him. I guessed then what had happened, and made Leek find a man, possibly a crook, who'd disappeared and who at some time or other had had all his teeth pulled out. We found the man who answered this description, a feller called Bert Liddy.'

'Who was the man who broke in, and what was he searching the desk for?' asked Norma.

'The man was Roone,' replied the stout detective, 'but what he was searchin' the desk for, I'm not sure, although I can give a pretty good guess. It's my opinion that he'd kept an account of the fire at Brighton in that secret drawer and forgot to take the newspaper cuttin's with him. He didn't want 'em found, and so took the risk of comin' back for them.'

'Well, you seem to have worked it out pretty well, Superintendent,' remarked Austin Barllard, rising to his feet. He looked at his watch. 'I'm going along to my solicitors to destroy that will,' he said with a chuckle.

'And if you make another,' remarked Mr. Budd, yawning, 'leave your money to the Society for the Prevention of Nicotine Poisonin'. You'll find it much safer!'

GRIM DEATH
MURDER IN MANUSCRIPT
THE GLASS ARROW
THE THIRD KEY
THE ROYAL FLUSH MURDERS
THE SQUEALER
MR. WHIPPLE EXPLAINS
THE SEVEN CLUES
THE CHAINED MAN
THE HOUSE OF THE GOAT
THE FOOTBALL POOL MURDERS
THE HAND OF FEAR
SORCERER'S HOUSE
THE HANGMAN
THE CON MAN
MISTER BIG
THE JOCKEY
THE SILVER HORSESHOE
THE TUDOR GARDEN MYSTERY
THE SHOW MUST GO ON
SINISTER HOUSE
THE WITCHES' MOON
ALIAS THE GHOST
THE LADY OF DOOM
THE BLACK HUNCHBACK

We do hope that you have enjoyed reading this large print book.

Did you know that all of our titles are available for purchase?

We publish a wide range of high quality large print books including:
Romances, Mysteries, Classics
General Fiction
Non Fiction and Westerns

Special interest titles available in large print are:
The Little Oxford Dictionary
Music Book, Song Book
Hymn Book, Service Book

Also available from us courtesy of Oxford University Press:
Young Readers' Dictionary
(large print edition)
Young Readers' Thesaurus
(large print edition)

For further information or a free brochure, please contact us at:
Ulverscroft Large Print Books Ltd.,
The Green, Bradgate Road, Anstey,
Leicester, LE7 7FU, England.
Tel: (00 44) **0116 236 4325**
Fax: (00 44) **0116 234 0205**

THIS IS THE HOUSE

Shelley Smith

On a picturesque West Indies island, the capital is dominated by the house on the mountaintop: the house that Jacques built. Premier Justice Antoine Jacques was divinely happy with his beautiful wife Julia and their son Raoul — until Julia was stricken with total paralysis . . . For years now, La Morte, as she is known, has been confined to her bed. Then, one day, she is found dead. And Quentin Seal, author of detective stories, is begged by Antoine to investigate . . .

THE SNARK WAS A BOOJUM

Gerald Verner and Chris Verner

When William Baker is found dead, his naked and twisted body lying under a bench in the dingy waiting room of a train station, the village police are baffled. Soon afterward another corpse appears, this time posthumously stuffed into full evening dress, with black pigment smeared on his face. A murderer is at large whose M.O. is to use his victims to recreate scenes from Lewis Carroll's nonsense poem, 'The Hunting of the Snark' — and it's up to amateur detective Simon Gale to stop him before he kills again.

JUNGLE QUEST

Denis Hughes

For several months, the British and European security agencies in Africa have been intercepting coded secret radio messages that are being received and responded to by a radio station hidden in the almost impenetrable depths of the Congo jungle. It's clear that some dastardly international plot is afoot. A top agent is despatched to investigate, but his reports cease abruptly, and weeks pass without further communication from him. So renowned jungle explorer Rex Brandon is hired to head an expedition to locate and neutralise the danger . . .

FIND MY SISTER

Norman Firth

When private investigator Al Maclean rescues Gail Grant from being assaulted in her hotel room, he has no inkling that she will become his next client. Gail is searching for her sister, who mysteriously disappeared from her hotel room two years ago, and Maclean's brief is simple: *Find my sister!* But his task is far from easy, as it turns out to involve criminal menace and murder . . . And in *Arrest Ace Lannigan!*, the star reporter of a London paper is out to bust a ring of American hoodlums terrorising the country.

THE CELLAR AT NO.5

Shelley Smith

Mrs. Rampage lives alone, in a large house cluttered with her precious objets d'art. Her daughter is half a world away, and her niece has no time for the old lady. So Mrs. Rampage is persuaded — much against her will — to take a companion into her home: Mrs. Roach, a poor but respectable widow. As resentment mounts between the pair, a violent confrontation is inevitable when the suppressed tension finally boils over . . .

SHERLOCK HOLMES AND MR. MAC

Gary Lovisi

'Mr. Mac', as Sherlock Holmes calls him, is the talented young Inspector Alec MacDonald. Though he's out to make his mark at Scotland Yard, some baffling new cases have him seeking assistance from the great detective; and the two, along with the stalwart Doctor Watson, join forces. In *The Affair of Lady Westcott's Lost Ruby*, the seemingly mundane disappearance of an elderly lady's pet leads to unexpectedly sinister consequences, while in *The Unseen Assassin*, a mysterious marksman embarks upon a serial killing spree across London.